DANNY ORLIS
AND
KENT GILBERT'S
TRAGEDY

DANNY ORLIS

AND

KENT GILBERT'S TRAGEDY

BERNARD PALMER

Danny Orlis and Kent Gilbert's Tragedy
© 2024 by Bernard Palmer
All rights reserved. First edition 1967.
Second edition 2024.

Scripture quotations from The Authorized (King James) Version. Rights in the Authorized Version in the United Kingdom are vested in the Crown. Reproduced by permission of the Crown's patentee, Cambridge University Press.

Cover image: Adobe Firefly

Character illustrations: John Ball

Editor: Jon D. Fogdall

Aneko Press Youth

www.anekopress.com

Aneko Press, Life Sentence Publishing, and our logos are trademarks of Life Sentence Publishing, Inc.
203 E. Birch Street
P.O. Box 652
Abbotsford, WI 54405

JUVENILE FICTION / Religious / Christian / Action & Adventure

Paperback ISBN: 979-8-88936-036-0
eBook ISBN: 979-8-88936-037-7
10   9   8   7   6   5   4   3   2   1
Available where books are sold

CONTENTS

CHAPTER 1

BAD COMPANY

Kent Gilbert shoved his cap back on his head and swaggered out the door of the junior high school and down the steps. Stub Taylor and the guys should be along from high school any time, he thought. Maybe they'd take him along with them again. It wasn't every guy his age who got a chance to go around with a bunch like that. They were tough. They didn't take anything from anybody.

When he saw them coming, he crossed the street.

"Hi, Shrimp," Stub said.

Kent grinned up at him.

"Hi."

"What're you doin' here?"

"Waitin' for you guys."

"Waitin' to burn a smoke, I suppose."

Kent looked around uneasily. He wanted to light up a cigarette like they did. They didn't care who saw them. But he didn't dare. Not out here, anyway. Not where everybody could see him. Danny would find out about it before he got home and he'd really be in trouble.

"Here," Stub said, taking a cigarette from the crumpled pack in his shirt pocket. "Now, don't say I never gave you nothin'."

"Thanks. Thanks a lot."

Buford Sellers and Carl Fredricks walked ahead of Stub and Kent.

"I've got the barn all lined up for the big party next Friday night," Stub said to Carl after a time.

"Great."

"Now, all you've got to do is get the beer."

"Don't worry about that. I've got a guy who'll buy it for us. All he wants for his trouble is a six-pack to keep for himself."

"Fair enough."

Kent's eyes widened. "What kind of a party are you guys having, anyway?" he demanded.

Stub laughed. "Just what kind of a party does it sound like, anyway?"

"Boy, it sounds great."

Stub reached over and rumpled the younger boy's hair with his hand.

"Now don't go gettin' any big ideas, Shrimp," he said. "You're too young even to be thinkin' about goin' on a beer binge."

"Oh, Danny and Kay wouldn't let me out at night," he said defensively. "They think I'll get hurt in the dark or something. But I'd like to help you guys. I could help clean the barn and get ready for the party, couldn't I?"

There was a short silence.

"Sorry, Shrimp, but not this time," Stub told him.

"Aw–"

Stub turned to his companions. "What do you think? Do we dare let him help us?"

Buford shook his head. "Nothin' doin'. He's liable to forget himself and let something slip that would get us all in a peck of trouble."

Kent bristled. "You don't have to worry about me lettin' anything slip. I know how to keep my mouth shut."

Carl spoke up quickly. "That's good. You'd better keep your mouth shut about what you've heard this afternoon, if you know what's good for you."

"I've already told you," he retorted, temper flashing. "You don't have to worry about me. I wouldn't squeal on anybody." He looked at Stub. "You tell 'em, Stub. You know I'm not a stool pigeon."

"You're OK, Shrimp," the youthful ringleader said. "You're plenty OK."

Kent grinned happily.

They liked him. They actually liked him. That should show that stupid Jim Morgan he could have some *real* friends, and they weren't the kind of guys who were getting into trouble with the law, either. They weren't like Jack Ross and his bunch, stealing tires and hubcaps and anything else they could lay their hands on. That was for the birds. Stub and his friends were swell, and they liked to have him around.

Slowly he walked down the alley, smoking the half of a cigarette Stub had given him. It burned his mouth and throat and made him cough a couple of times, but he didn't let that stop him. Someday he was going to talk them into taking him down to the old Finnegan barn with them. And when he did, he had to be able to smoke without showing how much it bothered him.

* * *

The following Sunday Kent went to church with Danny and Kay. He scooted down in the seat beside the missionary pilot, a scowl twisting his young face.

"Kent." Danny spoke in whispers. "Sit up."

"What're you kickin' about?" he demanded. "I'm here, ain't I? What more can you expect out of a guy?"

For an answer Danny grasped him firmly by the shoulder and pulled him upright.

"For cryin' out loud," Kent complained in a loud whisper. "Can't I even sit without havin' you nag at me?"

Danny frowned sternly at him. Kent knew what that meant and he fell silent. When that look came on Danny's face, a fellow didn't push anymore. He'd come to the end of the line.

The pastor preached on an old familiar theme. Kent tried to tune him out of his mind as he did so often, but on this occasion he could not. The words kept

hammering into his heart. The wages of sin is death! The wages of sin is death! *The wages of sin is death!*

He had heard that quotation often enough, but this was the very first time he had ever realized that it applied to him.

The preacher was talking to him that morning – Kent Gilbert. It was as though he was the only one in the congregation and the man who was speaking knew everything he had ever done or thought of doing.

Verse after verse of scripture came thundering from the pulpit.

"For all have sinned and fall short of the glory of God. There is none righteous, not even one. For the wages of sin is death, but the free gift of God is eternal life in Christ Jesus our Lord. For God did not send the Son into the world to judge the world, but that the world might be saved through Him."

Kent's entire being was aflame and for an instant or two he felt as though he could not keep from getting to his feet and going down to the altar. But he stubbornly resisted. He wouldn't take a stand for Christ and have guys like Stub and Buford and Carl make fun of him. Determinedly, he steeled himself against it.

Kent was strangely quiet for the rest of the day, and that night when it came time to go to the evening service, he tried to pretend that he had such a headache he couldn't go. But Danny would not permit him to stay at home.

"I think you'd better go anyway, Kent," he said.

"With a headache like this?" Kent demanded. "I tell you, I can hardly stand it!"

"The service tonight will only last a little over an hour. I think you can stand it that long."

The boy's face grew dark.

"OK. If you want me to go there and suffer. OK. I just wish you had a headache half as bad as this one and somebody made you go someplace. You'd know what it's like."

Danny did not answer him.

The next day after school the Gilbert boy again waited for Stub and his buddies.

"Hi, guys," he said when they came up.

Stub was the first to speak to him. "Hi, Shrimp," he said. "What's new with you?"

"What's new with you?" he asked, a knowing grin lighting up his young face. "How'd the party go?"

"Party?" Stub stared blankly at him. "We don't know what you're talking about. What party?"

"You know. The one you were going to hold in Finnegan's barn."

"Who said we were having a party in Finnegan's barn? I don't know anything about any party in Finnegan's barn, do you guys?"

Carl shook his head. "Nope," he said. "Not me. I never heard anything about having any party in Finnegan's barn."

"You did, too," the boy protested. "You were talking about it a few nights ago. You said you were going to have this big party in the barn on Friday night. A guy was going to get you some beer and everything."

Stub laughed scornfully. "You must have us mixed up with somebody else, Shrimp. We weren't going to have any party in any barn."

Kent's temper flared. "I don't know what's the matter with you guys. You act like I'm a stupid creep or somethin'."

Stub put his hands on his hips and stared down at the boy. "We can't help it that you get so shook up about things that you start to have dreams about a party in some barn."

Carl spoke up. "We're sorry, Shrimp, but it's not our fault."

Kent's eyes met his, belligerently.

"You guys know you told me about a party," he persisted. "You said you were goin' to have it in Finnegan's barn." He paused and lowered his voice. "You don't have to keep it a secret from me. I'm not goin' to squeal on you."

Buford laughed shortly. "You probably never kept a secret in your whole life."

"That's what you think. I've kept plenty of secrets."

"Name one."

"I'm not goin' to tell you."

"You're just talkin' now, Shrimp," Stub told him. "You've got to prove to us that you can keep a secret before we'll believe you."

Kent hesitated.

"Well–well–"

"That doesn't sound like any secret to me."

"You never heard about the secret of the lost silver mine in Colorado, did you? I never told anybody but you."

Scorn flickered in the older boys' eyes.

"Now, wait a minute," Stub countered. "Wait a minute. Don't try to sell any story about any lost silver mine, Shrimp."

"I don't care whether you believe it or not. I helped find a lost silver mine out in Colorado."

"You must've been having some bad dreams, Shrimp," Stub taunted, "to come up with a story like that one."

"I tell you, I did help find a lost silver mine," he repeated. "And I did keep it a secret – at least, I never told anybody but you guys about it."

"You shouldn't have told us now, Shrimp. Until today we figured you were always a truthful little guy," Carl told him.

"That's right," Stub went on. "I'll bet you haven't even been to Colorado, let alone back in the mountains far enough to help find a lost mine."

Kent's voice raised. "I did, too," he said. "You can ask Danny if you don't believe it. Only I don't think he knows anything about the mine. I never told him."

"And I don't think anybody else does, either," Stub went on.

Kent's mouth opened and he started to retort quickly, but he checked himself.

"Look, Shrimp," the ringleader went on, "you don't even know what a silver mine looks like."

"I do too." Kent stopped suddenly and fished several dynamite caps from his pocket. "Look at these, if you don't believe me. I got 'em in the mine."

Skeptically Stub examined one of them. His companions looked over his shoulder.

"They don't look like so much to me," Buford said.

"That's all you know about it. They're genuine dynamite caps!"

Stub's gaze met Carl's. Deliberately, he winked.

"You don't expect us to believe a story like that, do you?" he put in. "You can't fool me, Shrimp. I've seen hundreds of twenty-two blanks before."

Exasperation colored Kent's voice. "This isn't a twenty-two blank," he snorted. "It's a genuine old miner's dynamite cap. I picked it up from the floor of an old mine way back in the mountains behind Pikes Peak."

Stub handed back the caps and patted Kent on the shoulder.

"That's all right for you to believe those are dynamite caps if you want to, but don't tell that to anyone else. They're apt to think you're touched or something."

The boy's face colored.

"They are dynamite caps!" he cried. "Here, I'll show you!"

He drew back his arm suddenly and threw one of the caps on the cement sidewalk as hard as he could.

"Look out!" Stub jumped frantically to one side. But nothing happened.

The older boys laughed. Slowly a blank, hurt look crossed Kent's young face.

"But I–I know it's a dynamite cap. I just know it! I found it in the old mine!"

Buford nodded with mock sympathy.

"Oh, sure. Sure," he said. "If you tell us it's a dynamite cap, it's a dynamite cap, old buddy. We'll believe you!"

Speculatively, Kent picked up the cap and held it between his thumb and forefinger. They were making fun of him. That's what they were doing. They didn't believe he was telling the truth.

CHAPTER 2

KENT'S ACCIDENT

Back home that night Kent stood before the mirror in his bedroom, the ache growing in his heart. Stub and Buford and Carl didn't really like him. They just let him come around so they could make fun of him.

He drew the dynamite caps from his pocket and looked at them, his eyes clouding. They didn't even believe he had a couple of real live dynamite caps. And when he threw one of them on the sidewalk, the stupid thing didn't go off. That only made matters worse. Now they thought for sure that he was lying about being in Colorado and everything.

His fingers tightened around the brass objects in his pocket. He'd show 'em! He'd show 'em that he was telling the truth! He didn't know how, but he'd do it.

At that moment Danny called him to dinner. He shoved the dynamite caps into his pocket and remained motionless before the mirror.

"Kent," Danny called a second time, "dinner is waiting for us."

"OK! OK! You don't have to get in such a sweat about it. I'm comin'!" He sauntered out the door. "If you're so anxious to eat, go ahead and eat. I guess I can get along without it."

Nobody answered him.

As he sat down at the table, Jim Morgan looked up. "Hi Kent."

The younger boy scowled.

"What're you laughin' at?" he demanded.

"Nothing. I was just speaking to you."

"I'll bet you were just speaking to me," Kent said irritably. "I'll just bet that's what you were doin'. You act as though you think you've got something on me."

Danny's gaze met Kent's in disapproval. The boy fell silent.

* * *

The next morning Kent managed to be loitering near the high school when Stub and his friends came by. He spoke hesitantly.

"H-h-hi, fellows," he said.

"Hello, Shrimp."

Buford laughed. "Don't you know his new name, Stub?" he asked. "It isn't Shrimp. He's the Dynamite Kid!"

Carl snorted. "The Dynamite Kid! How about that!"

Kent's face flushed scarlet. "You guys think I don't

know what I'm talkin' about when I tell you I found a lost silver mine and got some old dynamite caps out of it, but I ain't foolin'. I'm tellin' you the truth."

"Sure," Stub said. "We know that, don't we, guys? We know you wouldn't try to feed us a line. You're too truthful to do a thing like that."

"Tell us, Kid, have you found any more silver mines?"

"Haven't you heard?" Carl put in. "He's found a lost silver mine in his own backyard."

Kent jerked the dynamite caps from his pocket and thrust them out. "Take a look at 'em!" he exclaimed. "Just take a look at 'em! And then tell me if they aren't real!"

Stub's laugh was tantalizing. "Sure. They're real enough. Real genuine twenty-two blanks. That's what they are. Anybody would know that."

At that moment, the older fellows walked away and left him. For the space of a minute or so he did not move. His face was livid, and his small fists clenched convulsively.

He was still standing there when Lee Nelson, a Christian friend who had been to camp in Colorado with him, came up.

"Hi Kent," he said.

Scowling, Kent turned to face him and grunted a greeting.

"What you got?" Lee asked.

"Nothin'." He shoved the dynamite caps back into his pocket.

"Going to be at the young people's party tomorrow night?"

"I don't know. It all depends."

"On what?"

"On whether that stupid Danny Orlis makes me go or not."

* * *

That evening shortly after dinner there was a knock at the Orlis door and Danny went to answer it. Lee was standing there. He was one of the boys who had gotten into trouble with Kent and Jack Ross the year before, and had accepted Christ as his Savior at Bible camp. Danny smiled warmly.

"Hello, Lee," he said. "Come on in."

The boy did not move.

"I–I'd like to," he said at last, "but I–I just came over to–to talk to you for a couple of minutes."

"Certainly." He opened the door a little wider. "Come on in. We might as well talk while sitting in a comfortable chair."

"I'd better not. You see, I promised Dad that I'd just run over here and talk to you a little while, then I'd come home and–and get at my homework." There was a short silence. "If I come in, I'm afraid I'll stay longer than I'm supposed to."

Danny stepped outside and closed the door behind him.

"And what is it you wanted to talk to me about?"

The towheaded lad did not reply immediately. He ran his fingers through his hair and looked up at the tall missionary pilot.

"I–I don't know whether you've any extra time to spare or not, but I–I've been doing a lot of thinking lately." He paused for a moment. "And I've been talking to some of the guys at school. We–we–" He swallowed with difficulty. "We'd like to have a Bible club like you have for the high school kids."

Danny's eyes lit up.

"You would?" he exclaimed.

"If–if we'd had a Bible club or something like that a year or two ago," Lee continued, "we might not have gotten into the jam we did with Jack Ross and–and have to be put under parole and everything."

Danny nodded.

"You're probably right about that. Bible study has a way of changing lives."

"Then–then it's OK?"

"I should say so," Danny replied. "I think it's a great idea. I'd like to encourage you to go ahead with it. And if there's anything Kay and I can do to help, you can count on us."

By this time, the younger boy was smiling. "If you'd teach it for us," he said, "that's all we'd need. We'll take care of everything else."

Danny reached out impulsively and patted him on the shoulder. "I'm pretty busy, Lee," he said, "but

I couldn't turn down a request like that. I'll be glad to teach your club. I'll expect you to do the inviting, though, and get the kids to come out."

"I've been thinking about that, too," Lee said. "Do you think Kent would come?"

Danny's expression changed. "I don't know," he said thoughtfully. "It's hard to figure out what he would do. But I'd sure appreciate it if you would ask him, Lee."

"Sure thing. I've been working on him already."

* * *

Kent, however, was giving little thought to anything except Stub and his friends at that particular moment. All they wanted to do was make fun of him, he thought. They really didn't like him. They just wanted someone to laugh at.

But he'd show 'em! He'd show 'em, all right!

Kent took the dynamite cap from his pocket, and for a brief moment, he held it between his thumb and forefinger. If it went off, they'd find out he really had been in an old silver mine in Colorado and had picked up some dynamite caps for souvenirs. They'd soon find out that he wasn't a phony.

He set a dynamite cap on the dresser and fingered the others in his pocket. Even if he did explode one of them, he'd still have the others. The trouble was the caps were so old they probably wouldn't go off at all.

Uneasily, he returned the dynamite caps to his pocket. He was going to stop those guys from laughing at him. He didn't know how, but he'd think of something. He was going to see to it that they didn't make fun of him anymore.

The next morning Kent went to school a little earlier than usual. He reached the place where he usually waited for Stub and his friends, keeping one eye on the sidewalk up the street. But they didn't come along. He waited there until he was almost late for school and still, they didn't come.

It was not until that afternoon when classes were dismissed for the day that he got to see them. As they approached, he grinned impishly up at them.

"Hi, guys," he said.

Buford sneered derisively at him.

"If it isn't the Dynamite Kid!"

That did it! The corners of Kent's mouth twitched, and his voice took on new determination.

"You think I've been lyin' to you about bein' in an old silver mine and finding dynamite caps, but I'll show you! I'll really show you!"

He took one of the caps from his pocket and threw it on the sidewalk as hard as he could. It bounced harmlessly away.

The boys laughed scornfully.

"Now, don't try to make us think that thing's actually goin' to explode," Buford said. "Anybody can take half a look at it and tell that it's just a big fat fake."

The boy's face was pale and anger gleamed in his eyes.

"If you think it's a fake, watch this!"

He dropped the dynamite cap on the sidewalk at his feet and, picking up a large stone, he drew back and fired.

There was a savage explosion that threw bits of stone and metal into the air.

Kent screamed!

CHAPTER 3

DR. HEALY'S DIAGNOSIS

Wildly, Kent screamed again.

Stub bent over the boy and seized him frantically by both shoulders. "Kent!" he cried. "What happened? What's the matter with you?"

By this time Buford and Carl had pushed close and were staring down at the screaming pain-stricken boy.

"What is it, Stub?" Buford demanded. "What's the matter with him?"

For the space of a minute or two Kent continued to cry out, covering his eyes with both hands.

"Kent!" Stub exclaimed. "Kent, are you hurt? Answer me!"

The woman who lived in the house on the corner had run out on the porch at the sound of the explosion. Now she dashed down the walk and knelt beside the injured boy.

"What happened?" she asked. "What is it, son?"

Stub acted as spokesman, speaking hurriedly, as though he feared she would blame him and his companions for what had happened.

"He's been carrying these dynamite caps around for a long time and showing them to us," he said. "A minute ago, he threw one on the sidewalk and it didn't go off. Before we could stop him, he picked up a rock and threw it at the cap. The thing exploded when he was practically on top of it!"

The woman gasped.

"There now, son," she said, turning her attention once more to him. "It's going to be all right. Tell us where you're hurt."

Kent's lithe young body stiffened and when he spoke his voice was still almost a scream.

"My eyes!" Agony broke his thin, terror-stricken voice. "My eyes!"

Gently she grasped his wrist and pulled his hand away. Her face went pale at what she saw, and for an instant she could not speak. At last, she turned to Stub.

"Who is he? Where does he live?"

"His name's Kent Gilbert, but he lives with some people by the name of Orlis on the other side of town." The words caught in his throat. "The little guy's hurt bad, ain't he?"

Decisively the woman got to her feet. "We've got to get him to a hospital right away."

"What'll we do, call the ambulance?"

She shook her head. "His burns seem to be around

his face. I don't think we'll hurt him by taking him in my car. While I get it, call the hospital and tell them that we're coming."

"When you've called the hospital," she said, raising her voice, "call the people he lives with and tell them what's happened. Tell them that we're taking the boy to the hospital."

The woman started for her car, but Buford stopped her.

"You don't have to bring the car over here," he said. "I'll carry him." Stooping, he easily picked Kent up and took him to the garage attached to the house.

Kent's screaming subsided somewhat by the time Buford got him to the car.

She backed out of the driveway after Stub jerked open the back door and scrambled in.

"Mrs. Orlis said she'd meet us at the hospital."

Kent still covered his eyes with his hands. His thin young body was hunched in the corner of the seat and his shoulders shook uncontrollably.

"I–I can't see anything," he mumbled.

Stub tried to comfort him. "You're going to be all right. When we get you to the doc, he'll fix you up as good as new."

The muscles in Kent's throat grew taut.

"I-I-"

The woman drove as fast as she dared through the streets of Fairview and up to the side door of the hospital. Two orderlies came out with a long cart. Buford had opened the car door and turned to reach in for Kent, but one of the hospital attendants touched him on the shoulder.

"Here," the orderly said, "let us take him."

Silently they got Kent out of the car, placed him on the cart, and one of them started to wheel him inside. The other turned to Stub and his friends. "What happened to him?"

Buford spoke defensively. "He was playing with an old dynamite cap. We didn't think it would go off, but–but–" Suddenly he was unable to find words to continue.

They wheeled Kent into the emergency room and pulled the door shut behind them, leaving Stub, Carl, and Buford alone in the hall.

"That poor little guy," Stub said in a hoarse whisper. "I sure didn't think that dynamite cap was going to explode. I thought it was too old to go off."

Carl took a deep breath.

"So did I."

Buford crossed the gleaming hospital corridor to the door where he stood for a minute or two, staring blankly out into space.

"You–you don't suppose they'll try to blame what happened on us, do you?"

Stub shook his head. "I don't see how they could. It wasn't our fault that he kept trying to get that dynamite cap to go off. It wasn't our fault that he picked up that rock and threw it at the cap. We didn't tell him to do it."

"That's for sure."

"M-maybe he isn't hurt as bad as we think he

is, anyway," Stub said, striving desperately to find hope in the situation. "You know something like this always looks a lot worse than it is before they get the guy cleaned up."

In the emergency room Dr. Healy had just finished giving Kent an injection to dull the pain and was completing his examination. Kay was standing silently nearby, her face pale, and concern dulling her eyes. By the time the doctor had finished working with Kent, the injured boy had lost consciousness. Slowly the doctor straightened up and turned to Kay. He motioned her outside.

"I gave him a stiff injection of morphine," he said, "and I think he's sleeping soundly, but there's a chance that he could wake up and hear snatches of what we're saying."

"Will he be all right, doctor?" she asked fearfully.

"This was a flash burn, but they can be as serious as any other kind of a burn," he said. "Apparently the boy was standing directly over the dynamite cap when it exploded. His eyes and the entire upper half of his face are badly burned.

Kay gasped. "The woman who brought him here told me that he kept screaming about his eyes."

The nurse who had been assisting the doctor motioned to the orderlies who came and wheeled Kent down the corridor to a private room. Not until he had disappeared from view did either Kay or the doctor speak again.

"Of course, it is his eyes that make this all so terribly serious."

"Is there any chance that Kent will lose some of his sight?" she asked.

Their gazes met evenly.

"Mrs. Orlis, this is most difficult for me to tell you," he went on, "but I don't believe the boy will ever see again."

Kay caught her breath. Perspiration came out on her forehead, and for a moment or two she swayed as though she would fall. The doctor stepped forward quickly, taking her by the arm.

"Are you alright?"

She did not answer him directly. "It can't be," she exclaimed. *It just can't be!*"

The doctor waited quietly.

"Isn't there anything that can be done?" Her voice was choked. "Can't you operate?"

"I'm afraid not."

Kay groped her way over to a chair and dropped, exhausted, into it. For the space of a minute she said nothing. Her lips trembled and she dabbed at her eyes. At last Dr. Healy spoke again.

"Would you like me to call your husband?"

She looked up gratefully. "Please."

"Would he be at the airport?"

"I think so."

Dr. Healy got Danny on the phone and told him about the accident and the apparent extent of Kent's injury.

"Tell Kay I'll get to the hospital just as fast as I can."

When the doctor ended the call, Kay smiled her thanks to him.

Dr. Healy went into the side office and got his coat and hat. On the way out he stopped once more beside Kay.

"The boy is under such heavy sedation he'll undoubtedly sleep all night. You should go home and get some rest. There's nothing you will be able to do for him by staying here.'

"Thank you, but I have to talk to Danny first."

"Of course."

"Dr. Healy," Kay said as he turned to leave. "Couldn't we call in an eye specialist?"

He paused momentarily.

"Tell me something, truthfully. Would you feel better if an eye specialist examined him?"

"I think I would."

The doctor drew in a long, thin breath. "My own judgment tells me that there's nothing anyone can do for the boy, except to treat his burns and make him as comfortable as possible. But I believe that if he were a child in my care, I'd want a specialist to examine him – just to be sure that everything possible had been done to save his sight."

"Thank you, doctor," she said simply.

"I can call Dr. Fordon if you want me to," their family doctor went on, "and tell him you are bringing the boy in for an examination."

"I'm sure Danny would want to do that, too, but I think it would be better to wait and talk with him about it first."

The doctor moved once again toward the door.

"You can call me at home as soon as you've decided, and I'll make all the arrangements for you."

It was only ten minutes or so, but it seemed to Kay like a day before Danny came running up the hospital steps and into the waiting room where she was standing.

"Kay!" he cried. "How is he?"

"Oh, Danny, he's not good," she said, her voice faltering. "He's not good at all." Several times she choked as she related the accident and told him what the doctor had said.

Perspiration stood out on Danny's forehead. He wiped it away with his muscular hand.

"Is there anything a specialist could do?" he asked.

Kay's eyes lit up. "That's the very question I asked Dr. Healy. He said he didn't think so, but that he'd make arrangements to call in a specialist if we want to."

The youthful missionary thought for a moment.

"I've got a lot of confidence in Dr. Healy," he said. "But even though it's only one chance in a thousand that a specialist could do something for Kent, I think we should take it."

CHAPTER 4

A DISAPPOINTMENT

Danny took out his cell phone to call Dr. Healy.

"What did he say?" Kay asked.

"He's going to call Children's Hospital in Minneapolis, Kay. Then he'll have an ambulance come and pick up Kent and take him out to the airport. I'll go on ahead and get the plane gassed and ready to go."

"Danny." Kay's voice was thin and small. "I want to go along."

He paused at the door.

"What about Jill?" he asked. "And Jim? Who'll take care of them while we're gone?"

"I could call Elsie Penner and see if she would take care of Jill for a day or so, and I'm sure Jim will want to stay at Pastor Reeves' house."

"Fine. You can come out to the airport with me."

She hesitated.

"Danny, I–I think I'd better ride in the ambulance with Kent. If he should waken, I–I'd like to be there."

* * *

That evening shortly after six-fifteen, Alex Smith walked in the door of his home. His young wife Robin had been home for almost two hours. She had finished her homework and was in the kitchen fixing supper when he came in.

"Hi, sweetheart." He went over and kissed her on the cheek. "Hey, what're you so sad about?"

"Did you hear what happened to Kent Gilbert?" she asked him.

Alex shook his head. "Now who's Kent Gilbert?" he wanted to know.

"The boy who lives with Danny and Kay Orlis. You know him, Alex. He's the younger one."

"Oh, sure. He's the little demon."

"The radio announcer just said that he was burned in some kind of an explosion accident and that Danny and Kay are flying him to Minneapolis to a specialist."

Alex sat down at the table, his young face looking serious. "That's too bad."

"They say it's his eyes."

Her husband frowned. "That would be terrible to have something happen to your eyes, wouldn't it? I'd just as soon be dead."

Robin felt the tears escape her eyelashes and trickle down her cheeks. "The poor little guy."

"I guess we don't know when we're well off, do we?"

"I was thinking that myself." She opened the oven, removed the baking dish, and set it on the table. "We think we've got it hard," she went on, "but our problems are nothing compared to what Kent might have to go through."

There was a brief silence.

"I can't help feeling sorry for him," Alex went on. "Even if he is a little stinker."

They talked for several minutes until the news came on. Robin broke off the conversation in the middle of her sentence and listened.

"Nothing more has been learned about the Gilbert boy who was flown to Minneapolis late this afternoon to be treated by an eye specialist for serious eye burns resulting from the explosion of a dynamite cap."

"Robin," Alex said, "please pass the meat."

She did not answer.

His voice raised. "Robin, please pass the meat."

She started suddenly. "I–I'm sorry, Alex. I was listening to the news."

"If you're going to try to save the rest of that meat for another meal, I'm telling you it's not going to work. I'm going to have another helping right now."

She passed him the meat dish and poured him another glass of milk. Concern still clouded her young face.

"Alex," she said, "is–is there anything that can be done for badly burned eyes?"

He looked up at her.

"Are you still worrying about that kid?"

She nodded.

"He's so young. When I think that he might be blind for the rest of his life, I feel so badly I–I can hardly stand it."

"Don't let it shake you so much. You hardly know him."

There was another long silence.

When Robin finally spoke, her voice was trembling.

"Right now, I feel as though I've known him all my life."

Alex reached across the table and covered her hand with his. "I think that's one of the things that makes me love you so much, Robin. You're so tenderhearted. I believe you'd take in every orphaned kid and cat in town if you had the chance."

She pulled her hand away. "Now, Alex," she said, "you're making fun of me."

"I'm not making fun of you. I'm just telling you the truth. That's all."

For the space of two or three minutes neither of them spoke.

* * *

The next morning when Robin and Alex got to school, they found that kids all around the building were talking about Kent.

Linda Penner was standing just inside the door, tears trembling on the edge of her eyelashes.

"Robin," she said, "have you heard the news?"

"About Kent?"

The other girl nodded. "I heard it."

"The Bible club kids are getting together for prayer a few minutes before school starts this morning, and again this noon. Would you like to join us?"

"Oh, I'd love to."

Alex's lips were crimped in a thin, mocking smile.

"You talk as though you really believe in that stuff, Robin." He spoke softly so only she could hear what he had said.

"I do believe it," she replied. "I believe it with all my heart. I've seen too many cases of answered prayer not to believe it."

Alex's smile faded and a strange note crept into his voice.

"Well, you can join in their prayer meeting if you want to, but don't expect me to come with you."

* * *

Danny and Kay left Kent at Children's Hospital and found a hotel room not far away. Neither of them slept much that night. They lay in the darkness of the little room talking or staring intently up at the ceiling, waiting for the time to go by.

Kay did not even want to eat breakfast the next morning before going to the hospital, but Danny insisted on it.

"I don't think I could eat a bite," she said. "Besides, I want to get over to the hospital right away."

Danny glanced at his watch. "It's only seven-thirty," he told her. "And the doctor isn't due to examine him until nine. We've got plenty of time to eat and get over to the hospital before then."

"But Danny," she protested, "I couldn't eat anything."

"We've got to keep our strength up if we're going to be of any help to Kent. Don't forget that."

She allowed him to guide her down to the hotel coffee shop. After they had placed their order, Kay spoke once more.

"I didn't sleep very much last night, Danny," she said.

"Neither did I."

"I kept praying that Dr. Healy would prove to be wrong, and that there will be something Dr. Fordon can do to help Kent have even a little vision."

Danny toyed with his spoon.

"It's not going to be easy for Kent if this diagnosis of Dr. Healy's proves to be correct."

Kay gasped.

"Danny!" she cried. "Don't say that! Don't even think it!"

As soon as they finished breakfast, they left the hotel and made their way to the hospital.

"We could take a cab, Danny," Kay suggested.

"We've got plenty of time," he answered. "If you aren't too tired, let's walk."

"I suppose that would be just as well. When we

get there, we'd just have to stand around waiting for the doctor to finish."

They paused at the corner and waited for the traffic light to change.

"Why do you suppose Kent exploded that old dynamite cap, Danny?" she asked after a time.

"I don't know for sure, but I've got a hunch those older boys had something to do with it."

"What do you mean?"

"You know how Kent has always wanted to run around with older fellows. I think he may have been trying to impress them."

"That could be." She sighed heavily as they started across the street. "Where would he have gotten a dynamite cap in the first place? We've never had anything like that around the house. Why, I hardly knew there was such a thing until yesterday."

Danny shook his head.

"I don't know where he could have gotten it. I've been trying to figure that out myself. A few years ago he could have picked one up almost anywhere around Fairview. Practically every farmer kept a box of them and a few sticks of dynamite for clearing stumps off new land they wanted to farm. But now bulldozing is so much better, cheaper, and faster that nobody uses dynamite anymore."

Kay pulled in a long, deep breath.

"I keep thinking this might not have happened if I'd just kept a closer watch on Kent," she replied miserably.

"Don't say that," he countered. "We both did the very best we could. That's all anyone can do."

She tightened her grip on his arm. "I don't think I've ever felt so miserable, Danny – or so helpless."

They went up the hospital steps and into the waiting room. When Danny introduced himself to the receptionist at the desk she consulted her notes.

"Dr. Fordon went up to Kent Gilbert's room a few minutes ago," she said. "He asked me to have you wait for him in the second-floor lounge. He'll go there as soon as he's completed the examination."

Danny and Key went up the stairs and made their way to the lounge where they were to meet Dr. Fordon. It was empty, except for a dour little gray-haired man who slouched in a corner, staring off into space as though he did not quite know what was happening.

At first Danny tried to pretend he was reading a magazine, but that was no good. The words swam before his eyes and Kent's burned young face stared up at him from every page. Kay was crying silently. Tears trickled, unheeded, down her cheeks. Every now and then she closed her eyes and prayed. Neither of them knew how many times they looked at their watches.

"I–I don't think I've ever known time to go so slowly."

"Or an examination to take so long," Kay added.

But finally, a tall, balding doctor made his way down the corridor to the place where they were sitting. As he approached, they both stood, automatically.

"Are you Mr. and Mrs. Orlis?" he asked.

"That's right. You must be Dr. Fordon."

Smiling gently, the eye specialist held out his hand. "I'm very glad to meet you both."

Kay broke in quickly.

"How is Kent?"

The smile fled from Dr. Fordon's kind face.

"Won't you sit down?" He seated himself across from them.

They did as he suggested, tensely.

"I wish I had some good news for you."

Kay sucked in her breath sharply.

"You mean—"

Dr. Fordon paused.

"The burns he suffered were very severe. The corneas of his eyes are completely destroyed. And, in addition, his eyeballs are badly cut from bits of flying stone or metal from the case of the dynamite cap."

"Is—isn't there anything you can do?" Danny asked.

Dr. Fordon shook his head.

"I'm afraid there is nothing anyone can do. You can only guess how hard it is for me to say this, but the boy will never see again."

Kay stared at the specialist, her young face pale.

"Are—are you sure?"

"I wish I wasn't." His gaze met hers. "Frankly, after reading Dr. Healy's report I was quite sure there was nothing that I could do for Kent. However, I have checked him carefully to be positive. His sight is completely gone."

It was some time before either Danny or Kay spoke again.

"Doctor," Danny said at last. "Does Kent know it yet?"

The specialist frowned. "I'm not sure, of course, but I doubt it very much. He's been under sedation since the accident. And, of course, his face and eyes are heavily bandaged. He may have some vague concern about his eyes, but I doubt that it's anything more than that."

"What about telling him?"

"That's something I want to talk with you about, Mr. Orlis. I don't think he should know for a few days – at least until he's a little stronger." He straightened up slowly. "But of course, the boy is going to have to be told quite soon."

"Would you like to have me tell him?" Danny asked.

The doctor shook his head. "It would probably be better if I tell him. I can explain to him exactly what happened and be there in case he goes into shock. However, I would like to have you and your wife in the room when I do."

"We'll be there."

After a time, Kay spoke nervously.

"What about seeing him now?"

The specialist pursed his lips.

"You can use your own judgment on that, Mrs. Orlis. I would like to point out one thing that may not occur to you, though. If he is awake when you see him, the first thing he's going to do is to start questioning you about his eyes."

"That's right," Danny said. "He'd really be after us, and we couldn't lie to him."

"Whether you lie to him or not is a personal matter, but at the moment, he's in no physical condition to be told that he'll never be able to see again."

Danny thought for a moment.

"In that case, Dr. Fordon, I think it would be best if we go back to Fairview without seeing him. That way we won't risk telling him something he shouldn't know yet. We'll keep in touch with the hospital and leave our phone number so you can get in touch with us when you want us to come back."

"Fine." Dr. Fordon got to his feet. "I think you are wise to go back. There's nothing you can do for him by staying here. That will all come when you get him home." He paused. "There'll be plenty for you to do for him then."

Kay swallowed against the lump that came up in her throat but said nothing.

"I'll be phoning you when I want you to come back. As far as I can see now, it will be toward the middle of next week." He shook hands again. "Oh, yes, there's one more thing. This is a little out of my field, but the boy's face is so badly burned that he'll have to have extensive skin grafts."

"I see."

"I suggest you have your local doctor make arrangements for a specialist in that field to see him in about a week."

"Thank you. We'll do that."

Danny guided Kay slowly down the steps and out into the warm spring morning. It was a bright, pleasant day, but neither of them were aware of it.

"Want to walk?" Danny asked. "Or should we call a cab?"

"I don't care." Her voice was dull and listless.

"Maybe it would be good for us to walk."

"Whatever you say."

Danny tried to talk to her as they made their way back to the hotel, but she answered in monosyllables or not at all. In the lobby they stopped at the desk when the clerk spoke to them.

"And how is the boy this morning?"

Kay burst into tears.

* * *

Danny and Kay flew back to Fairview that afternoon and drove over to see Pastor Reeves and to get Jim. Danny told the pastor what they had learned.

"But I think we should wait until Kent has been told before we let the story get out here in Fairview," he said, "if that's possible."

"I don't think you're going to be able to keep it a secret, Danny. Our phone has been ringing ever since you left. Everybody's been calling to find out how Kent is."

"I suppose you're right." He sighed wearily. "I

guess it doesn't make much difference. It's only a matter of a few days."

After stopping at Henry and Elsie Penner's for Jill, Danny and Kay went home. They had only been there a short time when the phone rang.

"This is Mr. Collins at the Welfare Office. Are you going to be home for a little while?"

"I think so," Danny said.

"Fine. I'll be right over."

Kay came into the living room. "Who was that?" she asked.

"The county welfare officer. He's coming over to see us."

The welfare director must have been ready to leave his office immediately. It seemed that he was at the Orlis home before Danny had time to set his phone down. Mr. Collins came into the house and sat in an easy chair near the door.

"That was a terrible thing that happened to Kent Gilbert," he said. "Terrible."

Danny nodded in agreement.

"Yes, Kay and I were both stunned by it. We haven't come to the place yet where we really believe it's true."

"I can well imagine." His voice was kind. "Those of us in our office have been so very grateful for the way you've been working with Kent and Jill. We've felt that they have made good progress in the time they've lived with you."

"With the Lord's help, we've done our best."

"If every couple who takes foster children into their home had the same concern for them that you have had for Kent and Jill, I'm sure the program would be much more successful than it is."

Mr. Collins straightened up in the chair.

"We've appreciated your concern for Kent in flying him to Minneapolis in the hope that a specialist there could help him. Most of our foster parents would have called us and told us to take care of him."

Kay's face clouded.

"Oh, we couldn't do that. We had to do what we could for him."

"I'm sure you did. And in my book, it was a very generous gesture." He paused. "I just stopped by to tell you that you won't have to worry about Kent from now on."

Danny eyed him curiously.

"What do you mean?"

"I mean that we feel we should take him back again. And Jill, too, if you want us to."

Kay gasped. "Oh, no!"

"Mr. Collins," Danny said, "you aren't serious about that, are you?"

"Now that Kent is blind," the welfare officer said, "there's going to be a great deal of time and expense involved in taking care of him. We'll have to take him back and place him in an institution. It wouldn't be fair to you not to."

Kay's face flushed. For a moment or two she

stared blankly at the welfare officer who was sitting across from her.

"You don't mean that, Mr. Collins," she repeated numbly. "You–you aren't serious about taking Kent away from us now, are you? Not when he needs us the most."

"We've discussed this at length, Mrs. Orlis," he repeated. "It's the only thing that's fair to you. You've gone to a great deal of trouble and expense for Kent already, and there's going to be much more. This is a responsibility that should rightly be assumed by the state."

Danny spoke up.

"Frankly, I have been quite concerned about the medical expenses that are being built up. We would be glad to pay them if we could, but on a mission-ary's salary–" he gestured expressively.

"We understand."

"Couldn't some arrangement be made for the state to assume the added expense and let him stay with us, Mr. Collins?"

There was a brief silence.

"I'm sure you haven't thought this through, Mr. Orlis. Kent has been a difficult boy to handle even before this happened. How do you think it's going to be to try to make him mind and become a respon-sible citizen now that he's blind?"

"I think he could make that adjustment in our home better than he could with strangers or–or in some sort of an institution," Kay said.

"What Kay says is right. You can't take him away from us now," Danny said. "Not when he needs us so badly."

The welfare officer eyed them incredulously. "I can't make you people out. Am I to understand that you actually want to keep the boy in your home *now,* after the terrible thing that's happened?"

Danny and Kay spoke almost in unison. "We certainly do."

Mr. Collins shook his head in disbelief.

"Now I've heard everything."

Their cuckoo clock struck five. No one spoke until it had finished calling out the hour. Then Danny spoke.

"You wouldn't force us to give up Kent, would you?"

The welfare officer was some time in answering.

"I can't give you a firm answer about that at the moment. It's something that we will have to consider very seriously. However, I assure you that we will go over the entire matter and give every consideration to your request."

"Thank you, Mr. Collins."

"We want to do what is best for Kent and for you."

Kay thought for a moment.

"Mr. Collins," she said, "we'd like to keep Kent. During the next few months he's going to need a lot of love, care, and kindness. And in spite of his problems, we do love him very much."

She started to cry.

CHAPTER 5

KENT'S REACTION

Several days later, Danny and Kay were just getting home from a committee meeting at church when Danny's cell phone rang.

"Mr. Orlis," the voice said. "This is Dr. Fordon at Children's Hospital in Minneapolis."

"Yes?"

"Could you and your wife come over the first thing in the morning? I think Kent is ready to be told."

Danny hung up and went into the living room where Kay was sitting.

"That was Dr. Fordon," he said.

"I know." Her face was pale. "Does he think Kent is strong enough to be told now?"

Danny nodded.

There was a long, thoughtful silence.

"I know what the doctor said," Kay continued at

last, "but I don't think he's the one to tell Kent that he'll never be able to see again."

"Neither do I." Danny was clasping and unclasping his hands nervously. "I'd rather take a beating than do it, but it might be easier for Kent if I were the one to tell him. I think I'll talk to Dr. Fordon about it when we get there tomorrow morning."

Kay was breathing heavily.

"Do you think you can?" she asked seriously. "Tell Kent, I mean?"

He stood, and for the space of a minute stared across the room as though his own eyes were sightless.

"I can't do it in my own strength, but if it will be easier for Kent, I can trust God to give me the courage and strength to tell him."

The following morning they left the house before daylight and Danny had the plane gassed and checked out by the time it was light enough to fly.

A few minutes after nine that morning Danny and Kay, together with the doctor, went into Kent's room. At the sound of their footsteps Kent sat up straight.

"Who is it?" His voice raised peevishly. "Is that you, Doc?"

"Who else would be calling on you so early in the morning?"

"Are you going to take the bandages off my eyes today, Doc?" the boy persisted. "Are you?"

The specialist hesitated briefly.

"I've brought someone to talk to you, Kent," he said.

"I don't want to talk to nobody." Desperation crept into his voice. "I just wanna get these stupid bandages off so I can see."

Kay stifled a sob and Danny frowned his disapproval at her.

"Hi, Kent," he said as brightly as he could manage.

"Danny!" Excitement gripped him. "Am I ever glad you came!"

"We've sure been thinking a lot about you," he went on. "And praying for you, too."

Kent expelled his breath slowly.

"It's good to have you here."

By this time Kay had regained her composure enough to speak.

"Hello, Kent," she said. "How are you?"

"Kay!" Incredibility crept into his voice. "You came, too?"

"Nobody could have kept me away."

Danny spoke up in the silence that followed.

"How're you feeling now, Kent?"

"I'm OK," the boy answered. "If the doctor would only take these stupid bandages off so I could see. I'm tired of this."

Kay started to cry once more, silently. Danny pulled up a chair and sat down. Prayerfully he sought for words.

"I was talking to the doctor on the way up here to see you."

"You were?" The boy's voice rose. "Did he say

anything about getting these bandages off, Danny? I can't watch television or read or anything."

For the space of a minute or two there was no sound in the little hospital room except the labored breathing of the occupants. At last Danny scooted his chair closer to the bed and took Kent's hand in his own. His voice was husky with emotion.

"Kent, how brave are you?"

Slowly the boy lowered himself to rest on one elbow.

"Wh–what do you mean?"

"The doctor tells me that you are going to have to be very brave."

Kent started to speak, but it was some time before he could force out the words.

"It's not going to make any difference when they do take off these bandages," he said. "I'm still not going to be able to see, am I, Danny?" His voice broke. "Am I?"

Scalding tears welled up in Danny's eyes and the muscles in his throat tightened convulsively. But when he spoke his voice was normal.

"The doctors have done all they could, Kent," he went on, "but the dynamite explosion burned your eyes so severely that they weren't able to help you."

Kent turned his head away from Danny and sank back on the pillow.

"I won't be able to see." His voice was hollow and expressionless. "I'll never be able to see again!"

* * *

That afternoon Danny and Kay went back to the hospital to see Kent. He was lying in the same position he had been in that morning. His lithe young body was rigid and his small fists clenched. If he heard them enter the room and close the door, he gave no sign. Kay approached the bed and leaned over him.

"Kent," she said softly.

He did not move.

"Kent, we came back to see you."

Nothing about him changed.

"Do you feel all right?"

Both of them tried to talk to him, but it was no use. He would not respond. At last Danny motioned Kay out into the hall.

"It's no use, Kay," he said. "He isn't going to talk to us."

"I've never felt so sorry for anyone in my whole life."

A deep sigh escaped Danny's lips.

"Neither have I," he said, "but we've got to get through to him somehow, if we're going to be able to help him."

Kay moved a few feet away from the door. "He always has resisted our efforts to get close to him. Now it seems as though he's built a shell a foot thick around himself."

They walked half the length of the corridor before either of them spoke. At last Kay glanced in Danny's direction.

"If only he knew Christ as his Savior," she said, "it would be so much easier for him to take a blow like this. He'd have a source of strength besides himself."

Her young husband nodded. "I was thinking the same thing. I guess I half expected something like this from Kent. He's always been so rebellious."

"I've thought of that, myself. But it doesn't make it any easier." She breathed deeply. "If we only knew what to do now."

Near the elevator Danny stopped.

"I think I'll go in and see the doctor for a minute, Kay," he said.

"Right now?" Her reluctance was obvious.

"If you don't care to go with me, you can stay in the waiting room."

She forced a thin smile to her lips.

"If you don't mind, I think I'll wait for you, Danny," she said. "I–I don't feel very much like talking with anyone right now."

They took the elevator to the main floor. Danny went back to the doctor's office while Kay found her way to the waiting room and sat down.

Kent was blind. It still didn't seem possible. At any moment she would wake and find that it had all been a terrible nightmare. Poor Kent. He had always been so headstrong – so belligerent. What would happen to him now?

Kay closed her eyes and prayed silently until Danny came out.

"Did you get to see him?" she asked.

He sat down beside her.

"Only for a minute. I wanted to find out how Kent's been doing."

"What did he have to say?"

"I guess Kent hasn't eaten anything or spoken a word to anyone since we talked to him this morning."

"The poor boy!" Kay wiped at her eyes with a tissue.

"The doctor seems to think this is a natural reaction."

"What did he have to say about our going in to see him again this evening or tomorrow?"

"He felt that it would be better if we go back to Fairview for a few days so that we won't be visiting Kent."

Kay gasped.

"And leave him here alone?"

"He said that we're too close to Kent, that we would tend to sympathize too much with him."

She bristled.

"I've never heard anything so heartless. I don't care what that doctor says. I'm not going to leave him. He needs us now more than he has ever needed us in his life before."

"Right now, Kent needs to accept the fact that he is blind and will never see again." Danny spoke gently. "If we sympathize with him, he's not going to make that adjustment as rapidly as he will otherwise. That's what the doctor means. He's thinking of Kent's welfare."

Kay got uncertainly to her feet.

"Maybe he's right, Danny," she managed to say, "but I–I don't think I can stand it back in Fairview knowing that Kent is here all alone."

"We've got to think of what's best for him."

There was a brief period of silence.

"I know that, Danny. And I–I do want to do what's best for him."

"The doctor thought it would be much better if we wait until the first of the week to come back to see Kent. The doctors and nurses have had experience in dealing with cases like this. They know better than we do what should be done."

Kay allowed her young husband to guide her down the steps and out into the street.

CHAPTER 6

UNDER CONVICTION

Danny wanted to get back to Minneapolis and visit Kent the first of the week, but an emergency at one of the mission stations in Canada would take him north for ten days or so. Kay was greatly disturbed.

"Danny," she said, "you can't go and leave Kent in the hospital alone at a time like this. He needs you."

"I know that, but the mission needs me, too. I'm the only one who can fly these supplies in."

Her lower lip trembled.

"Couldn't you explain to them about Kent and see if they could wait?"

Danny put his hands on her shoulders.

"Kay," he said, "I feel as badly about Kent as you do. But it just isn't possible for me to change things now. Besides, you'll be here. You can go down to see him."

"It isn't just seeing him that I'm thinking about." She spoke slowly. "Ever since this tragedy, I've been praying that he would accept Christ." She pulled in a long, deep breath. "But I feel that it's going to have to be someone like you to talk with him. Someone he respects. He would never listen to me."

The missionary pilot thought momentarily.

"Pastor Reeves could go to see him for us."

Kay brightened.

"Do you think he would?"

"I *know* he would."

They called their pastor that evening and the next day he and his wife went to Minneapolis to visit the blind boy. Kent was lying motionless on the bed when the nurse showed them into his room.

"Kent," she said, "you have company."

There was no answer. Kent's slight form did not move. Neither did his heavily bandaged head. The nurse spoke once more.

"Kent!" Her voice raised. "You have company!"

"I don't want no comp'ny," he blurted.

The nurse turned to Pastor Reeves.

"I don't think he'll talk to you," she said.

"That's all right." The pastor's voice was kind and jovial. "We'll talk to him."

The boy turned on his side.

"You might as well beat it. I ain't talkin' to nobody."

The pastor and his wife sat down near the bed. After a time, Pastor Reeves spoke.

"Hello, Kent."

There was a long silence.

"I don't need a preacher," the boy said, snarling bitterly. "I can tell by your voice who you are."

"That's right, Kent," the pastor answered. "Mrs. Reeves and I are both here."

"Well, I don't have nothin' to talk to you about so you might as well get out of here."

Pastor Reeves talked as though he hadn't even heard Kent. He and his wife talked with the boy as casually as if Kent were entering into the conversation. They told him what was going on in Fairview, what the kids in his class were doing, and how the baseball team was making out. All the while he lay as rigid and immobile as though he were made of steel. Finally, Pastor Reeves changed the subject slightly.

"I saw Lee Nelson the other day, Kent," he said. "He was asking about you."

There was another short silence.

"As a matter of fact, he stopped by the study to ask me to pray for you with him."

The corners of Kent's mouth twitched.

"Why was he prayin' for me now?" he demanded.

"He's concerned about you, Kent," the minister said. "He's especially concerned since he learned about your accident. He's been praying for you ever since."

"And a lot of good it did!" Bitterness curled the boy's lips. "I'm still blind!"

"Lee hasn't been praying that your eyes would

be restored, Kent. He's been praying that you would accept Christ as your Savior. He's been concerned about your soul."

For the space of a minute or two there was no sound in the tiny hospital room except the labored breathing of the injured boy. At last Kent spoke.

"I got a letter from Lee a couple of days ago," he said. "One of the nurses read it to me."

As the pastor continued to talk a change seemed to take place in Kent's manner. It was so slight at first that it was scarcely perceptible. But as the minutes passed the boy began to open up a little. Once he even smiled.

When Pastor Reeves arose to leave, Kent held out his hand impulsively. "I sure am glad you came," he said, swallowing hard. "Outside of Danny and Kay, you're the only company I've had."

"That's because you're so far from home," the minister told him. "Why, if you were in the hospital in Fairview, you'd be having a lot of company."

"I'll bet." Some of the boy's bitterness came back again.

They were still standing there talking with Kent when the nurse came in and told them that visiting hours were over.

"We'll have to be leaving now, Kent," the minister said.

"You–you'll come back, won't you?"

"We certainly will." With his hand on the doorknob, he turned back. "I just thought of something, Kent. How would you like to have a radio here in your room?"

The corners of the boy's mouth twitched.

"It–it'd be better than television."

The minister acted as though he had not heard the burst of self-pity.

"I'll tell you what I'll do," he said. "The next time we come, I'll bring a radio for you. Then you can listen to some of the gospel programs."

* * *

That evening Lee Nelson stopped by the Orlis home to find out how Kent was getting along.

"Pastor and Mrs. Reeves will be coming back tonight." Kay paused in her dishwashing to answer his question. "I've been expecting them to come over anytime now and tell us about Kent."

Lee crossed the kitchen and sat down on a stool near the refrigerator.

"I wrote Kent another letter this morning," he said. "But I don't know whether to mail it or not. I haven't had an answer to the first one yet."

"Don't wait for that, Lee." Kay spoke quickly. "He may not write to you right away, but he needs all the encouragement any of us can give him."

"I just didn't want to write to him if he didn't want to get my letters."

"I'm sure he's had the nurses read your letter to him a number of times."

The slender lad's face grew serious.

"If he would only decide to live for God instead of himself, everything would work out a lot better for him," he said. "God would give him the strength he needs to take this blindness or any other problems he's got."

Kay nodded.

"Danny and I have said the same thing so often. It would be much easier for Kent if he would just accept Christ as his Savior." She paused momentarily. "We'll just have to keep on praying for him."

* * *

Back in Minneapolis in the Children's Hospital, Kent spent a great deal of time listening to the radio Pastor Reeves had brought him on his next visit. By this time most of the pain was gone and Kent was waiting for the skin grafts to take. The radio became his only source of entertainment.

If they had put it close enough to him, he probably could have operated it himself, but they had it on a stand some distance from his bed. And rather than have the stand moved closer to him, he got one of the nurses to take care of the tuning. He preferred the music on one station and listened to it all morning, but at noon he switched to another that regularly carried the baseball games. When the nurse's aide who brought him his lunch came in, he asked her to change stations for him.

"What station do you want to listen to?" she asked.

"I don't care what station you tune in, just as long as it carries the ball game."

She fiddled with the dial. "That's this station," she said presently.

He listened to it for a moment.

"Are you sure?"

"Of course, I'm sure." Her voice raised. "I'm a baseball fan myself."

He was silent for a time.

"You can sneak in here and listen awhile this afternoon if you want to."

"Oh, I can't do that. I've got my work to do," she told him.

"I won't tell on you."

"I might slip in as I'm going by, but I won't be able to stay for more than a minute."

At that instant, the music of a well-known Christian broadcast came on loud and clear. The woman's voice lit up.

"Oh, I listen to that program."

Kent's face clouded.

"Turn it off!"

"Don't you want to hear the game?"

"I don't care whether I get to listen to it or not," he snapped. "Turn it off."

She switched off the radio. He lay there waiting for her footsteps to indicate she was making her departure. But they did not come. After a time, he spoke once more, belligerently.

"Well, go on. Get out of here! What're you wait'n for?"

Her voice was gentle. "I was just wondering something about you, Kent."

"Like what?"

"Why are you so bitter against the Lord?"

The silence was deafening. For a full minute all that could be heard in the little hospital room was the boy's labored breathing.

"Why shouldn't I be?" His lips curled. "Just look at me! Just take a look at me!" Self-pity quavered in his voice. "God ain't done nothin' for me! He ain't *never* done nothin' for me!"

The nurse's aide picked up a dish and set it on the tray before him.

"God doesn't promise us an easy life, Kent," she said, her voice quiet and gentle. "There are a lot of things that happen to people that are really terrible, but that doesn't mean that God is breaking His word to us. All He promises is that He will give us strength and courage to face the things that come our way."

Kent swallowed hard. It was an effort for him to speak. And when he did so, self-pity and bitterness all but choked his voice.

"You can talk that way. You never had nothin' bad happen to you!"

She moved closer to him and laid a hand on his young arm.

"My husband died two years ago, Kent," she began, "and I had to go to work to support myself." She paused momentarily. "But that's not the hardest thing I have to bear. I have a son about your age. He was sick when he was less than a year old and his mind didn't develop anymore. He's in a mental institution now and will never be able to live anywhere else." There was no anger or self-pity in her manner. "It is true that I haven't known what it is to be hurt the way you are, Kent, but if I could trade places with my son so he could live a normal, happy life, I would do it gladly."

Kent was breathing so heavily that he could not speak at first. He swallowed against the lump in his throat and uneasily shifted his position.

"Are–are you sure the baseball game comes on after the Christian broadcast on this station?"

"I'll check the paper if you want me to," she said, "but I'm pretty sure it does. I listened to them both on my last day off."

Kent snorted indifferently.

"OK. Turn it on if you want to. But I'll tell you before you do that I ain't goin' to be listenin' to no radio preacher. I'll just wait for the ball game to come on."

When she closed the door behind her, he rolled over so that his back was to the radio and tried to go to sleep. But sleep would not come. He tried thinking about Jill, and Danny and Kay, and what it was like before the explosion blinded him, but it was no use. The words of the speaker drove deep into his heart.

It was the longest half hour he could remember spending since the skin grafts. Yet he clung desperately to what the speaker said. At last, the program was over and the ball game was on.

The Minnesota baseball team got in trouble in the first inning and were three runs behind. But they fought back in a desperate battle that finally brought them victory in three extra innings. Normally a game like that would have left Kent limp with excitement. However, on this occasion, he could not have cared less. He lay back on the pillow trying to listen to the music that followed. But the frenzied beat and discordant melody jarred his very being. With a swift motion he reached up and opened the intercom switch.

"Nurse!" His young voice was harsh. "Come in here and turn off this radio!"

That message he had just heard was no different than the things Danny and Kay had told him many, many times, or what Pastor Reeves preached. But for some reason it hit him harder than it ever had.

You must be born again! *You must be born again!* It drove to the very depths of his heart.

The next day when the nurse's aide came in to turn on the radio for him, he was ready for her.

"Just leave the thing alone. You can come back and turn it on about two o'clock."

"Don't you think it would be better to turn it on now?" she asked.

He raised himself on one elbow.

"Nope. I ain't listenin' to that radio preacher no more. And that's final."

Her voice changed.

"I wish you would listen to him, Kent," she continued. "Just this once."

He shook his head. "I got my fill of that yesterday."

"All right, Kent." The gentleness did not leave her voice. "If that's the way you want it." At the door she turned. "I just want you to know that I'm praying for you every day."

With that the door closed behind her.

For the space of a minute or two, Kent did not move. His sightless eyes were facing the wall and his fists were clenched.

Why did she have to go and say that? He didn't need anyone to pray for him. He'd always gotten along all right on his own. And he'd keep on getting along without any help from anyone. He'd get along somehow.

Kent's lips quivered and he started to cry.

A moment later the door opened.

"I'm sorry, Kent, I forgot my–" The words choked off suddenly. "Kent!" She moved silently to the bed. "What's the matter?"

He scrubbed at his eyes with his small fist.

"N–n–nothin'."

"There is something wrong." She took his hand gently. "Tell me about it."

"It's nothin', I tell you! Go on and leave me alone. I don't want you in here!"

The nurse's aide straightened up slowly.

"If you want me, just call."

He let her get almost to the door.

"Mrs. Hamilton?" he said, his voice weak.

"Yes?" She turned back.

"I really don't care if you turn on the radio."

"Now?"

"It's about time for that broadcast, ain't it?"

After that he listened to the Christian program every day it was on. The music was beautiful and he looked forward to hearing it. But he wasn't sure he liked the messages. Half the time he couldn't even sleep at night for thinking about what the preacher had said. The ache within his heart continued to grow as the days passed.

About a week later he was listening to the program when Mrs. Hamilton came in and told him there had been a call from Pastor Reeves.

"He wanted to know how you're getting along."

"He should know that."

"And he said that he and his wife will be here to see you tomorrow afternoon."

"What am I supposed to do?" Kent said testily. "Jump up and down and shout for joy?"

"I thought you enjoyed visiting with the pastor and his wife."

"Well, you've got another thing coming. There are a lot of things I like better than layin' here while someone preaches at me!"

CHAPTER 7

KENT'S DECISION

On the following afternoon Pastor and Mrs. Reeves came to Children's Hospital to see Kent. From their other visits the blind boy knew about what to expect from them. When they came into his room he had his back toward them, pretending to be asleep. The minister went over to the bed.

"Hello, Kent," he said.

"Perhaps he's asleep."

Mrs. Hamilton, who had come into his room with them, spoke up quickly. "I'm sure he isn't asleep. I was just in here a couple of minutes ago and he asked me what time it was."

Kent's lithe young body stiffened. If Pastor Reeves noticed, however, he gave no indication of it. Leaning forward, he tapped Kent on the shoulder.

"Kent?"

There was no answer.

"Kent?" His voice raised. "Kent, we've come to see you."

With obvious distaste the boy rolled over on his back, a scowl twisting his young face.

"What do you want?" Anger lay just below the surface in his voice.

"We just wanted to see you. How're you feeling these days?"

"All right, I guess."

The minister and his wife sat down near the boy's bed. For a moment or two there was no sound in the small white hospital room. At last Pastor Reeves broke the silence.

"How have things been going for you, Kent?"

"How have things been going for me?" he demanded, his bitterness surging back with a rush. "How do you think they've been goin'? I lay here on this stupid bed all day long. And if I don't like layin' on my back I can lay on my side. They'll even crank the bed up for me." His voice broke. "Big deal!"

"I'm sure they do the very best they can for you."

Kent opened his mouth to speak, but the minister kept right on talking. "Have you been listening to the radio I gave you?"

"A little." He spoke grudgingly. "I listen to the ball games."

"So do I – every chance I get." He leaned back in the chair. "And what about the Christian programs that come on over the Minneapolis stations. Do you listen to any of them?"

The boy's face clouded.

"Have you been talkin' to that stupid Mrs. Hamilton?" he demanded.

"Mrs. Hamilton?" the pastor echoed. "Who's she?"

"That dumb nurse who's always stickin' her nose into my room. Did she say anything to you?"

"I don't know who she is, but nobody here in the hospital has told us anything about you." He leaned forward curiously. "What was it you thought she might have said?"

"Oh, skip it."

The minister continued to talk to him – or tried to. But Kent seemed determined not to carry on a conversation. He refused to respond to anything that was said, except in answer to a direct question. Even then he only spoke in monosyllables. Mrs. Reeves also tried to draw him out, but without success. Finally, she turned to her husband.

"Don't you think it's about time for us to leave?"

He glanced at his watch. "I had no idea it was so late. We were having our car worked on, Kent, so we came in on the bus today. I suppose we'd better be leaving soon if we're going to get back to Fairview tonight."

Kent did not reply.

"The other day," the minister said, opening his Bible, "I was reading in the book of John when I came across some verses that I think would be an encouragement for you, Kent."

"I don't need nobody to read the Bible to me," the

boy protested curtly. "I've heard so much Bible the last couple of weeks that it's been runnin' out my ears."

Nevertheless, Pastor Reeves read a short portion to him and prayed. Kent did not protest, but an ugly frown stamped his face and the color drained from the portion of his features that wasn't bandaged. At last, the minister finished praying and got to his feet.

"We have to go now, Kent."

The boy did not reply.

"I think we'll try to come back again in a week or ten days."

Kent grunted something or other that was all but unintelligible.

Once they were out in the corridor Pastor Reeves turned to his wife. "Did it seem to you that Kent was acting especially strange this afternoon?"

She nodded.

"I thought he acted very strange," she replied. "Actually, he seemed worse than he has been at any time since the first visit we made."

"I was thinking the same thing, but that's not what I meant. It seems to me that he's bothered about something."

"Like what?"

They walked to the end of the corridor and started toward the elevator.

"I had the distinct feeling that Kent is under conviction."

Leaving the building they walked leisurely down the street in the direction of the bus depot.

"He didn't seem to be under conviction to me," his wife said. "Actually, I thought it was quite the contrary. He seemed so indifferent to anything spiritual. It was as though he didn't care at all."

They got back to the depot half an hour before their bus was to leave for Fairview. The minister started for the newsstand to buy a paper but came back and suggested that they go into the coffee shop.

"I think there's just time for us to grab a sandwich before our bus leaves."

She got to her feet.

"I'm not very hungry, but I would like to have a glass of iced tea."

They were served almost immediately and didn't waste any time – or so it seemed. But when they came out their bus was gone.

"But it can't be!" the minister exclaimed. "We've been right here in the coffee shop for the past twenty minutes. Wasn't the bus announced?"

The agent's voice was cold and impersonal.

"I'm sorry, sir," he said, "but your bus was announced ten minutes before departure and again just a minute or two before it left. Those announcements are piped into the coffee shop, so you should have heard them, even in there."

Pastor Reeves turned back to his wife.

"I can't understand it." He shook his head incredulously. "I just can't understand it. This is the first time in my life that I have missed a bus or train."

"Perhaps there's a reason for it."

His gaze met hers.

"What do you mean?"

"Are you forgetting what you told me about Kent a little while ago?" she asked him.

"You mean about his being under conviction?" His wife nodded.

"I don't know whether it has anything to do with our missing that bus or not," she said, "but it could have. God could be telling us to go back to the hospital and talk to Kent."

The pastor expelled his breath thoughtfully.

"There's got to be a reason why we missed that bus," he said. "I think you're right. I'll phone home and tell them we won't be back until tomorrow. Then we'll go back to the hospital and see Kent again."

When they got back to the hospital it was after visiting hours, but the pastor stopped at the desk and insisted on seeing the boy again.

"It's very important."

The nurse frowned.

"Will it take long?"

"I can't say. It may only take a minute and it may take a considerable amount of time. But I feel that I must see him tonight."

She studied the chart momentarily.

"It is against regulations, but I think it would be all right. I know the problems that poor boy has had." For an instant, her professional exterior cracked a little and she managed a thin smile. "You and your wife may go in."

"Thank you."

They walked down the corridor to Kent's room. As they stepped inside Kent turned quickly.

"Who's there?"

"It's only us, Pastor and Mrs. Reeves," the minister said. "We missed our bus this afternoon, so we came back to see you."

"Oh." His voice reflected his disappointment.

The minister and his wife pulled up chairs and sat down.

"As a matter of fact," he said, "this is the first time in my life that I have ever missed a bus or a train. It's so unusual for me that I honestly believe it happened for a special purpose."

"What do you mean?" the boy asked.

"I've been here to see you several times, Kent," he went on. Although he spoke quietly there was an urgent tone in his voice. "I've never really felt led to talk with you in a personal way about the Lord Jesus Christ until now. But ever since we left here earlier this afternoon, I've had such a burden for you that I've hardly been able to stand it."

Kent winced.

"You'd better get 'shook up' about somebody else, Pastor. You ain't hookin' me on religion. That's for sure."

If the boy was trying to make the minister angry, he failed completely.

"I don't want to 'hook' you on anything, Kent. This has to be a deliberate, voluntary act on your part." He paused significantly. "Tell me, Kent, have you ever considered the claims of the Lord Jesus Christ on your life?"

Kent raised himself on one elbow.

"Nobody's got any claims on my life! I can tell you that much right now. I do as I please."

"That's where you're wrong, Kent," Pastor Reeves went on. "The Lord Jesus died on the cross to save you from the results of your sin. That gives Him a very definite claim on your life."

Kent swallowed with difficulty.

"I–I–" His voice trailed thinly away.

"The question is this. What are you going to do about it?"

Kent tried to speak, but he could not. His lips were quivering.

"God loved you so much, Kent, that He sent His only Son to die on the cross for your sin."

"I never asked Him to," he blurted.

The minister leaned forward slightly.

"That's one of the most wonderful things about it all, Kent. God didn't send Christ to die for us because we asked Him to. He did it because He loves us so much. He wants to save us!"

There was a short silence.

"Won't you put your trust in Him?"

Kent moistened his lips with the tip of his tongue.

"God wouldn't save me," he said uncertainly.

"In the Bible He says He will. He says, 'The one who comes to Me I will certainly not cast out.'"

That did it. Kent burst into tears and yielded his heart to Christ.

CHAPTER 8

A NEW VISITOR

Pastor Reeves and his wife were so excited about Kent's decision for Christ that they called Danny and Kay from the hotel that night and told them about it.

"Praise the Lord!" Danny's voice broke. "That's what we've been praying for, for months."

"He came through in a wonderful way," the pastor said. "In fact, I don't know when I've talked with anyone who's made such a clear-cut decision."

Tears came to Kay's eyes when she realized what they were talking about. She went up and put her arm around Danny's waist, listening.

"The last thing Kent asked as we left the hospital a little while ago," the minister said, "was that we get word to you as soon as we could. He wanted you to know."

"That's tremendous news," Danny said. "I think we'll fly down tomorrow and see him."

Before they hung up, Danny made arrangements with the pastor and his wife to meet them at the hospital the next afternoon.

"And after we've seen Kent," he concluded, "you can fly back with us."

* * *

When Danny and Kay came into Kent's hospital room with Pastor and Mrs. Reeves, Kent was sitting up in bed listening to the baseball game. Danny strode up to the bed.

"Hi, Kent."

"Danny!" The boy's face lit up. "I didn't expect you today!"

"I'm here, too," Kay said. She came up and kissed him lightly on the cheek.

"Aw–" He protested weakly, but it was obvious that he wasn't nearly as annoyed as he pretended to be.

"Turn off the radio, will you, Danny?" Kent said.

"You don't have to turn it off on our account," the missionary pilot told him. "We enjoy listening to a ball game, too."

"I really wasn't listening much this afternoon," he said.

When the radio was off, he turned his sightless, bandaged face toward his guests. "Did you see Pastor Reeves this morning?"

"As a matter of fact, yes. He and Mrs. Reeves are here with us now."

The boy hesitated briefly.

"Did–did he tell you that I'm a Christian now?"

"He sure did. That's why we came down today. We're very happy about it, Kent."

"I should've done it a long time ago, when you and Kay first talked with me about it," he said, "but I just got mad instead."

"That's all right, Kent. We understand." He breathed deeply. "The important thing is that you have made your decision now. That you have accepted Christ as your Savior now and have the assurance that you are saved."

"I know I'm a Christian," the boy repeated. "That's for sure. I did just what Pastor Reeves told me to do. I told the Lord that I am a terrible sinner and was headed for hell unless He did something about it. I told Him I wanted Him to take over my life. That's it, isn't it?"

"That's right, Kent. When we admit that we are a sinner and trust Christ to forgive our sins, He makes us 'sons of God.'"

Kay reached over and took Kent's hand.

"We're so happy for you," she said. "So very happy."

* * *

Danny and Kay took Lee Nelson with them to Minneapolis the next time they went to see Kent. As they neared the hospital the boy squirmed uneasily.

"Wh–what's Kent like now, Danny?" he asked after a time.

The missionary pilot eyed him curiously.

"What do you mean, Lee?"

"Does–does he feel awful bad 'cause he can't see anymore?"

Danny's lips pursed thoughtfully.

"Yes, I think I'd have to say that he does. He probably feels worse about it than anything else that has ever happened to him. But, of course, it's a lot better now than it was before he was saved. Now we can show him that he can get strength and help from God. He'll have something to cling to besides himself."

Still Lee was not satisfied.

"This may sound silly to you, Danny, but there's something I'd like to ask you. H-h-how do you talk to a guy who's blind? What can a fellow say?"

* * *

Lee stood uneasily just inside the door of the hospital room.

"We've brought someone to see you, Kent," Danny said.

"Who is it? Pastor Reeves?" His face lit up briefly.

"It's somebody else. Somebody you wouldn't even think of. Would he, Lee?"

At the mention of the other boy's name the smile brightened on Kent's face.

"Hi."

"How're you feelin'?"

"All right, I guess." There was a brief, embarrassed silence.

"Boy, it–it sure is good to see you."

Kent's fingers worked nervously on the edge of the blanket. It seemed to be harder for him to talk with Lee than it had been to talk to anyone else.

"H-how're all the guys back in Fairview?" he asked.

The young guest shifted uneasily from one foot to the other.

"They're OK. At least 'most everybody is," Lee told him.

"I suppose they're all playing baseball now."

"Not everybody. Some of the guys can't play because they've got jobs for the summer, and Jim Morgan isn't playing because he went north to help Ron."

The Gilbert boy lay back on the bed, breathing heavily. When he finally spoke, his voice was thick with self-pity.

"I was going to try out as a pitcher this year," he said.

"Yeah, I know."

"I had to go to that camp in Colorado and didn't get to play last year, either. Now, I–I'll never get to play again."

"M-maybe you will," Lee said. He couldn't look at Kent. He was staring at the floor.

"N-no I won't! I'll never get to play baseball again!" Hot, scalding tears coursed down his cheeks and his shoulders twitched convulsively.

Danny stepped forward and took hold of his arm.

"Kent," he said, his voice stern. "Get a hold of yourself."

Lee looked at his young friend miserably.

On the way back to Fairview Lee was strangely silent. When he spoke, his voice revealed his concern.

"I had the idea that Kent would be glad I came to visit him, but he sure wasn't. He didn't act as though he wanted to see me at all."

"I'm afraid that having you come made Kent jealous of the fact that you can see and he can't," Danny replied. "This afternoon he was feeling very sorry for himself.'"

"I guess he's got a right to feel bad, if anybody does," Lee went on. "That'd be tough to have to go through life without ever seeing again."

Danny nodded.

"It would be tough, that's true. But nobody else can help Kent. He can't even help himself – as long as he's filled with self-pity."

They rode on for a mile or so before the boy spoke again.

"Did the doctor say when Kent will get out of the hospital?" he asked.

"If everything goes well for him between now and then I believe he'll be released in a couple of weeks," Danny said.

"Think he'll go to school this fall?"

"That's something I'm not sure about. I rather imagine he'll come home to stay for a while. Neither

Kay nor I want him to go away to a school for the blind until he's made a little better adjustment than he has so far."

Lee's lips pursed. "I suppose he will have to go to a special school. I never thought of that."

"I think he'll have to go to a school for the blind for a while," Danny said. "He'll have to learn to take care of himself and learn braille. I don't know whether he'd be able to go to a regular school after that or not. We'll just have to wait and see."

Lee nodded.

"He sure needs our prayers, doesn't he?"

JIM JOINS THE TEAM

In Fairview, school had already started. Lee, like most of the boys in his grade, went out for football. As he was awaiting his turn at the tackling dummy, he turned to the guy next to him. "What do you think of the new coach?" he asked.

"Coach Harper?" his friend echoed. "He's all right. It doesn't make any difference to him who a guy is or whether he made the team last year or not. All he cares about is how well he can play football."

Lee nodded.

"Of course, I don't figure on making the first string," he went on. "I'll be plenty lucky to get to play with the second team this year."

"Me too."

Lee's lithe young body tensed as he took his turn at the tackling dummy. He ran as hard as he could and plowed into the heavy dummy with his shoulder.

"No! No! No!" The coach's voice rose above the noise on the field. "That's not the way at all. Now watch how I do it, Nelson."

"Y-y-yes sir!"

When the practice session was over, the new coach came over to Lee.

"Lee, I was talking to some of the guys a minute ago," he began. "They tell me that you're a friend of this Jim Morgan who played on the team last year."

Lee took off his helmet and stood with it in his hand.

"Yes, he's a pretty good friend of mine."

"When's he going to show up in school?" the coach wanted to know. "Or is he?"

"Oh, he'll be back, all right. I thought he'd be here by now. He went up north to help Ron Orlis do some building on a mission station or something."

The coach frowned.

"I've been talking to some of the guys around town and they say he's pretty good." He paused momentarily. "I've been anxious to see if he can do all the things they say he can."

"Jim's good, all right. I don't think there's anyone better. At least here in Fairview High."

"If he doesn't get here before long, it's not going to make much difference how good he is; we won't be able to use him."

* * *

CHAPTER 9

As soon as Jim got back to Fairview and enrolled in school, he went out for football. At first, he had a few anxious moments. He didn't know whether Coach Harper was going to let him try out for the team or not.

"You're mighty late to join the squad, Jim," the coach said, picking up a pencil and toying with it. "The other fellows have been practicing for more than a week."

"I know that," Jim replied. "And I've been doing a lot of thinking about it, believe me. But we just couldn't get back any sooner."

The coach frowned.

"I've just about settled on my starting lineup. I suppose you're aware of that." His gaze met Jim's. "Tell me, are you willing to come out and practice with us without knowing whether you'll make the team or not?"

Jim spoke up quickly.

"Oh sure," he said. "I mean, yes, sir."

"And you'll play with the second team, if that's the best you can do?"

"I'll play with the second team," Jim assured him, "or–or do just about anything you want me to do. I just want a chance to play."

The coach got to his feet and for the first time he smiled.

"OK. I'll see that you get a uniform."

It was good to get out on the football field again, even though Jim didn't know for sure whether he'd get to play or not. The other guys had a distinct advantage over him. They had been working with Coach Harper for more than a week and were beginning to learn the plays and how to function as a team. Fortunately, Jim was in good shape from his summer's work at High Rock. His muscles were stone hard, and he was able to run and tackle with the rest of them.

He was getting dressed in the locker room after one of the practice sessions when a guy he didn't know came over and sat down beside him.

"Hi."

Jim looked up.

"Hi. I don't believe I know you." He grinned and thrust out his hand.

"I'm Fritz McCloud," the newcomer said. "I just moved here with my folks."

They finished dressing and walked out together.

"Well," Jim said, "how do you like it here in Fairview?"

"It's nothing compared to the place where we used to live. That's for sure."

In spite of himself Jim bristled noticeably.

"You'll like it when you get acquainted with more people. I felt the same as you do when we first came here, but I've never lived in a better town."

Fritz McCloud frowned.

"I don't think I'll ever like it."

Although Coach Harper had told Jim there was little chance of his getting into the game that Friday night, he did send him in during the closing minutes as blocking back.

The quarterback called for McCloud to carry the ball. It was a play very similar to one they had used the year before and Jim was familiar with his responsibility. At exactly the right moment he pulled out, came around and threw a savage block to spring the ball carrier for a touchdown.

A roar went up from the stands.

Grinning, Jim went back to his position. Fritz came over to him.

"Thanks."

In the dressing room after the game, Fritz sought Jim out once more.

"Got a way home?"

"Danny and Kay are here, but they won't want to wait until I've finished dressing. I suppose I'll just have to walk."

"How'd you like to ride with me?" Fritz asked.

"Great."

When they finished getting into their street clothes and went out to the car, Jim was surprised to see a girl sitting in the front seat. He stopped and turned to his companion.

"Hey, wait a minute. I didn't know you had a date. I don't have far to go. I can walk."

"That's not a date." Fritz took Jim by the arm. "It's just my sister, Connie. I tried to get out of hauling her around, but if I wanted the car tonight, I had to promise to give her a ride home from the game."

"I sure wouldn't want to interfere with anything."

"You're not." He lowered his voice. "We'll dump her off at the house and then go down to the drugstore for something to eat. How about it?"

"Sounds OK to me."

They went around the back of the car and approached the front door. Jim stopped, his eyes widening. The girl in the front seat was a vision of loveliness. Soft blond hair framed her delicate features and her blue eyes gleamed merrily.

She looked up at him and smiled.

That did it. His heart fluttered and his tanned cheeks flushed crimson.

"Hello," she said. Her voice was as friendly as her smile.

Jim tried to speak, but the words clung in his throat. His lips parted, but no sound came out.

By this time Fritz had opened the door on the other side and gotten in.

"OK, Jim," he said. "Hop in."

"Aren't you going to introduce us?" his sister asked.

"Oh, sure. Connie, this is Jim Morgan," he said. "He's the guy who threw the block that sprung me for that touchdown."

She eyed Jim demurely.

"I know," she said. "I asked one of the girls who you were."

Jim grunted something or other in response to the introduction, but still remained standing as though a sudden paralysis had seized him.

Fritz started the engine, and Connie slid over to make room for Jim in the front seat. Numbly he got in beside her.

Fritz had been watching him curiously.

"What's the matter, Jim? You sick or something?"

"Me, sick?" He sat up straighter and tried to laugh. "No, I'm not sick. There's n-nothing wrong with me."

* * *

On Monday morning Jim was walking to school when a car pulled up beside him and the door opened invitingly.

"Hello, Jim," a familiar voice said.

His heart stopped for an instant. There was Connie McCloud smiling at him.

"Hello," he managed to say.

Jim just stood there.

"Would you like a ride?" she asked, sliding over to make room for him in the front seat beside her.

He got in and closed the door. Fritz laughed as though he had just heard a good joke.

"I planned on going straight to school," he said, "but Connie insisted on driving over this way in case we happened to see you walking."

She blushed.

"Fritz!"

"Well, it's the truth, isn't it?"

Jim could scarcely believe what he heard. If she did that it must mean that she liked him – at least a little bit.

"It was sure nice to see you in church and Sunday school yesterday." He hadn't intended to say that. It just popped out.

Connie smiled up at him.

"Oh, we've been going to that church ever since we moved to town. The first thing we did when we got here was look for a good, gospel-preaching church."

He looked at her again.

"Then–then you must be Christians," he said.

"Oh, we are." Connie spoke quickly.

Jim looked at her again. She was not only the prettiest girl he had ever seen in all his life, she was a Christian, too. That meant that Danny and Kay would be sure to approve of her.

Fritz started talking, but Jim was only half listening.

"I was surprised when Dad told me that I could drive to school this week." He wheeled around a corner, paused at the stop sign and headed for the high school on the edge of town. "I've been trying to talk him into getting me a car of my own, but I didn't think I was getting anywhere at all until this morning."

"That'd be good, all right." Jim had scarcely any enthusiasm in his voice. He was trying to listen to Fritz and keep from looking at Connie all the time. It was virtually impossible for him to keep from staring at her. At last, he turned to her. "How–how do you like it here in Fairview?"

Before she had a chance to answer, Fritz spoke up.

"I don't mind telling you that I don't like it. I don't like it at all. It's the crummiest town I've ever been in."

Connie smiled.

"I think it's a real nice little town. In fact, I'm getting to like it better all the time."

"You are?" Jim brightened noticeably.

"Of course, I had a lot of friends back where we used to live," she went on, "and I hated to leave them."

He swallowed hard.

"I'm sure glad you did move here."

She smiled in his direction and a warm glow enveloped him.

When they got out of the car, somebody called to Fritz, so he left Connie and Jim standing together.

"Here," he said, "let me take those books for you."

Her reply was soft and musical.

"Thanks, Jim."

He took them from her and together they started up the walk to the school building. Jim knew what he wanted to ask her, but he couldn't bring himself to do so until they were almost at the front door.

"If–if you haven't met many of the kids," he said, "I–I'd be glad to take you around and introduce you to some of them. I mean, I'd–" His voice trailed away miserably.

"Why Jim, that's so thoughtful of you."

He grinned self-consciously. She must like him a little bit or she wouldn't look at him that way. That gave him the courage to ask her something else.

"I–I was just wondering, Connie," he stammered, "if you'd like to eat lunch with me at noon?"

Her forehead wrinkled thoughtfully, and for an instant her smile disappeared.

"I don't know for sure, Jim. I'll have to see about that at noon.

His heart fell.

The rest of the morning all he could think about was a tiny elfin face with blond hair and two smiling blue eyes. She might eat lunch with him, but that was almost too much to hope for. She would probably be with one of the big wheels in the junior or senior class, or with a flock of girls. She wouldn't want to spend her lunch hour with him.

But she did! She was waiting for him when he came down the stairs. As the two of them went into the cafeteria together, he could feel the envious gaze of the guys on him. He decided right then not to introduce her to anyone unless he had to. They'd have to get acquainted with her over his dead body!

CHAPTER 10

KENT'S HOMECOMING

That night at the dinner table Danny told Jill and Jim that Kent would soon be coming home. The blind boy's sister beamed.

"Oh, Danny!" she cried. "That's wonderful!"

Jim agreed.

"Boy, you can say that again. I can hardly wait until he gets back home. It seems as though it's been years since he's lived here."

But Danny was serious.

"I think Kay and I are as excited about Kent's coming home as you two are," he said, "but there's something that we are all going to have to remember."

The smile faded from the Morgan boy's face.

"Going blind has had a great effect on Kent." Danny explained. "He's got a big adjustment to make and is under a lot of strain. He might not be as easy to get along with as we would like him to be."

Both Jill and Jim eyed Danny curiously.

"But he's a Christian now, Danny," Jim said. "He'll look at things a lot differently than he used to."

"I'm sure he will. But you know, Jim, the fact that a fellow accepts Christ as his Savior doesn't make him perfect overnight. Kent is a Christian and he's trying hard to live the way a Christian should and to let Christ have complete control of his life. But there are times when he starts feeling sorry for himself. Then he isn't too easy to get along with."

Kay spoke up.

"It's our job now to try to help him make the adjustment so that he can get the most out of life. We've got to help him get control of himself and learn to take care of himself."

Jill was toying with her fork.

"I know everybody says there's a reason for everything that happens, but I can't see why it was Kent who had to go blind."

Danny nodded understandingly.

"I know just how you feel. We can't figure out why these things happen. I don't believe God wants us to even try to understand. We've got to learn to put our whole trust in the Lord Jesus Christ, even when we can't see His reasoning."

Jill's lower lip trembled. "I–I wish there was something we could do to help him."

"There is something we can do," Danny said. "Something we can all do. We can be understanding when he's cross and disagreeable, and we can be sure to pray for him every day, asking God to help him to accept what has happened and to learn to take care of himself and to make the most out of life in spite of it."

They had their devotions and spent a long time praying for Kent.

After they were finished and Jill and Jim were drying the last of the dishes, Jill spoke up suddenly.

"Jim," she said, "who was the girl I saw you with at noon?"

The color crept up into his cheeks. He glanced quickly at Danny to see if he had heard.

"Girl?" he echoed. "What girl?"

"You know the one." Disgust crept into Jill's young voice. "The one you were with at lunch. The pretty blond who's been to our church lately."

There was an embarrassing silence. Jim's face was fiery red. He folded and refolded the dish towel as though it was the most important job in the world. With exaggerated indifference he shrugged his shoulders.

"She was just a girl I happened to be standing beside in line, that's all."

Jill was not satisfied with that explanation.

"You were sure looking at her a lot. You looked at her so much you tripped over a chair and almost fell down."

A grin crept across Danny's face. "What is this, Jim?" he asked. "Maybe you'd better do a little explaining to the rest of us. This sounds like an interesting story."

"Aw–"

"She must be a new girl, Danny. I've only seen her the last few weeks."

"It wouldn't be the McCloud girl, would it, Jim?" Danny asked.

The Morgan boy looked up.

"For cryin' out loud! Can't a guy even stand in the cafeteria line with a girl without having to go through the third degree?"

Danny laughed.

"Sure you can. If it's all right with her dad, it's sure all right with me."

"She's just a new girl in town," Jim tried to explain. "I was just trying to be friendly so she wouldn't get lonesome."

"It sounds as though you were very friendly," Danny went on.

Kay caught Danny's eye and frowned her disapproval.

"Now, Danny," she said, "don't you think you've teased Jim enough? I think it's nice that he's found a girlfriend, and I'm so happy that she's a Christian."

"Oh, I'm real happy that he's found a girlfriend. He almost had me convinced that he didn't like girls. To tell you the truth, he sort of surprised me."

Jim swallowed hard. That Jill would have to go and tell on him. Now he'd probably never hear the end of it.

* * *

The following morning Danny and Kay flew to Minneapolis to pick up Kent. When they got there, he was dressed and waiting for them.

"Hello, Kent," Danny said. "Boy, you're looking great."

Briefly a smile lit up the blind boy's face. "I thought you were never goin' to get here."

"We wanted to come earlier, but I got in so late with the plane last night that I didn't have a chance to get it serviced until today. Are you all set to go?"

Kent nodded.

"I–I guess so."

The three of them went down the hospital steps together. Kent clung tightly to Danny's arm.

"You–you'll stay right by me, won't you?" he asked nervously. "You won't leave me, will you?"

"You don't have to worry about that," Danny assured him. "Kay and I both will be right here."

For a moment he seemed to relax a bit, but on the street he stopped. A strange look crossed his young face.

"Danny?"

"Yes?"

The boy swallowed at the lump in his throat.

"Danny," he repeated. "What's it going to be like when I get home?"

The missionary pilot eyed him quizzically.

"What do you mean?"

Kent was fumbling for words. "I–I won't have to go out and–and be with a lot of people, will I?" His voice broke. "I won't have to go around where everybody is talking to me about how I am and–and–"

"I'm sure people won't be talking to you much about yourself, Kent. At least not right away. If anyone does ask you how things are going, it will be because they're concerned about you and are interested in how you are making out."

Kent took a deep breath.

"I don't want to talk to anybody."

"We have to be around people, Kent," Danny told him. "Nobody can live alone. But it won't be so bad for you after awhile. Right now, the most important thing for you is to become adjusted so you can live as normal a life as possible."

Kent's expression did not change.

"I–I'm not going to go anyplace. When I get back to Fairview I–I'm just goin' to stay at home. I'm not goin' to go places and have everybody starin' at me."

Kay looked at Danny and winced. This was the thing they had been afraid of.

Danny changed the subject abruptly.

"Kay, you stay here with Kent. I'll go and get a cab. We should get back to the airport as soon as we can."

When he was gone Kent tightened his grip on Kay's arm. "You won't let Danny *make* me go out and be around people, will you?"

She did not answer him.

"Will you?" His voice raised.

"You'll want to be around your friends, Kent," she answered at last.

His young face twisted with bitterness and fear.

"I don't want to be around anybody! And I won't!"

Danny, Kay, and Kent got back to Fairview from Minneapolis that afternoon shortly after school was out. Jill was waiting for them, her eyes bright with excitement.

"Oh, Kent. I'm so glad to see you!" She threw her arms around him and hugged him.

"What've you been doin' since I've been gone, Squirt?"

"Nothin'." Tears came to her eyes. "I wanted to come and–and see you all the time, but I–I couldn't." In spite of herself she sniffled.

When Kent spoke, his voice was unnaturally harsh.

"Now, don't start blubberin'."

Her lithe young body stiffened. "I'm not."

"You sure sounded like it to me."

There was a brief pause.

"I wasn't really crying, but wh-what do you expect? A girl's brother doesn't come home from the hospital every day."

For half a minute or so Kent stood there, looking about with sightless eyes.

"I–I'd like to go to my bedroom for a minute and–and–" Words choked in his throat.

Helplessly Jill turned to Danny and Kay.

"I–"

"You can take him there if you'd like, Jill." Kay spoke tenderly.

"I–I can't!"

Quickly Danny got to his feet and grasped Kent's arm.

"Come on," he said. "I'll take you in there."

When they were gone Jill turned to Kay, sobbing miserably.

"Oh, Kay!" she cried. "It's so–so *awful!*"

Kay gently put her arm on the back of Jill's head.

"That's all right, honey," she said. "Cry if you feel like it. It will make you feel better."

There would be time later to talk to Jill about being brave in front of Kent and helping him to help himself. Right now the distraught girl needed the release of tears. She couldn't comfort Kent yet. She needed to be comforted herself.

They had supper and were still sitting at the table when several guys from Kent's Sunday school class stopped by. Lee was one of them.

"When we heard you were home we just had to come over and see you."

The blind boy's lips trembled uncertainly and he did not speak.

"We've sure missed you," Lee continued.

His companions nodded.

"We sure have."

Kent still could not reply.

"We just wanted to tell you that we've all been praying for you, Kent. We prayed for you every single night since–since you got hurt."

The expression on the blind boy's face softened.

"I–I sorta figured that you had been," he said. "Thanks. Thanks a lot."

"We'll be lookin' for you in our Sunday school class next Sunday, Kent. I'll be waiting on the steps for you Sunday morning so I can go to class with you."

"I–I don't know whether I'll be there or not," Kent answered uneasily. "I–I'll have to see how I feel Sunday morning."

They continued to talk for a few minutes, but Kent scarcely entered into the conversation, and it wasn't long before Lee and his friends left.

Once they were gone the blind boy got unsteadily to his feet.

"Danny." His voice was trembling. "Danny, if you'll take me into the bedroom, I think I'll go to bed."

The young pilot did not move immediately.

"There's something I've been wanting to talk to you about, Kent. I hadn't planned on going into this with you right away, but I think it's just as well that we do it this evening."

"I don't feel much like talking now," he replied.

Danny ignored his remark.

"This morning before we left the hospital I was talking to the doctor. He said that we should help you to find your way around the house and then let you learn to manage for yourself so that you won't be too dependent on anyone else."

Kent's lips quivered.

"That's all right for him to say, but he doesn't know what it's like not to be able to see!"

"He said you should be able to get around the house very well in just a little while," Danny continued.

Kent took a deep breath.

"If I'd known I was going to be treated like this when I got home, I'd have stayed in Minneapolis at the hospital."

Nevertheless, he started forward. Without saying anything more, Danny took him by the arm and guided him to the bedroom door.

CHAPTER 11

A HAPPY SOLUTION

The following Friday night there was another football game. It was a hard, bruising game with frequent penalties. Midway in the second period Paul Jackson, the blocking back who had won the starting position over Jim, was on the bottom of the pileup. When everyone else got up, he still lay there, stretched out on the grass. Coach Harper ran out onto the field. A couple of minutes later the team doctor helped Paul to the sidelines, and the coach came up to Jim.

"All right, Morgan; go in for Paul," he said crisply.

Jim peeled off his sweatshirt and dashed onto the playing field. On the very next play he knifed through the opposing line to nail the ballcarrier for a five-yard loss. That forced them to punt. And on the punt return he threw a block that made it possible for Fritz to pick up another eighteen yards. At halftime Fairview was leading, thirteen to twelve.

As they left the field at the half, Jim sought out the football coach.

"How's Paul?" he asked.

"He's got a bad sprain and a pulled tendon. I'm afraid he's going to be out for the balance of the season."

"Oh, that's tough."

Coach Harper eyed him critically.

"You really mean that, don't you, Jim?"

"Sure. Why?"

"I thought at first that you might be glad because it means that you're going to get to play, but I can tell by the look on your face that you are serious when you say you're sorry about it. I like that in a guy."

* * *

When the game was finally over, Fairview had added another touchdown to the one-point margin they had carried into the second half. Jim had played most of the third and fourth quarters and had done fairly well. The coach complimented him after the game.

When Jim left the school after showering and changing clothes, he saw Connie McCloud and went over to where she was standing.

"Hi," he said. "Looking for anybody in particular?"

Her smile was infectious.

"Just my brother."

"Why should you want to see him when you can talk to me?" he said.

She laughed happily.

"Who said I wanted to see Fritz?" she went on. "It's a ride home that I'm looking for."

"I–I was wondering if you would like to walk home with me?"

She hesitated.

"I don't suppose Fritz would care."

"You know Fritz wouldn't care," he assured her.

"I guess not. He's always complaining when he has to take me with him."

"Complaining about taking *you* with him?" Jim echoed. "He doesn't know how lucky he is."

"He doesn't think so."

They left school and headed toward town. It was a warm fall evening and they walked slowly, talking in low tones.

"Would you like to go down to get some ice cream or something cold to drink?"

"That sounds like fun." She paused for a moment. "I suppose I should have told Fritz where I'm going. He might wait at the school for me."

"I don't think he will," Jim said. In spite of himself a grin crept across his face. "I told him that if you weren't out there waiting for him, you'd gone with me."

"You did?" she exclaimed. "You must have been pretty sure of yourself, weren't you?"

"Not sure of myself," he answered. "Just hopeful."

Over ice cream in the drugstore that evening Jim told Connie about Danny and Kay and how he came to live with them. He even went into the story of Kent and told her about his losing his eyesight and the hard time he was having getting adjusted to it.

"It must be terribly hard on him."

On the steps of the McCloud home Connie thanked Jim for the evening.

"I don't know when I've had such a good time, Jim," she said.

A smile spread across his face.

"Neither do I. This has been great."

For a moment he stood there, shifting nervously from one foot to the other. Connie was about to go in but saw that he still had something to say to her.

"It's getting late," she said, "and my parents will be wondering what's keeping me. I really should go in."

Jim swallowed a lump in his throat and forced out the words.

"Do–do you think you'll be going to church next Sunday night?"

"Yes, I think so. Why?"

The color came up into Jim's cheeks again.

"I–I was just thinking that–that maybe if you'd like to, you could go to church with me Sunday night. That is, if you aren't afraid of somebody teasing you or something."

"Teasing me?" she echoed. "Why would anybody want to tease me about going with you?" Her smile was gracious and reassuring. "As a matter of fact, both Mother and Dad are glad to have me go with you because they know that you are a Christian."

He made no comment, but the same warm glow he had known before came over him. Her folks liked him, too. That was almost too much to hope for.

As Jim walked home, he felt as if his feet weren't even touching the ground.

* * *

On Sunday morning Danny and the rest of the family got ready to go to church and Sunday school, but Kent sat stubbornly in a chair in the living room. Danny, who had been taking a last quick look at his lesson, didn't notice that Kent was not dressed for church until Kay came in.

"Kent," she said, "you're not ready for Sunday school and it's almost time for us to leave."

His mouth tightened.

"I'm not goin'."

Danny closed his quarterly.

"We always go to Sunday school and church."

"What the rest of you do doesn't mean anything to me," he retorted, some of his old belligerence coming back. "I won't go."

Danny spoke up quietly.

"I think you'd better go and get dressed now, Kent," he said. "We'll have to leave in ten or fifteen minutes. We don't want to be late this morning."

The boy's voice raised.

"Then go ahead and go. I'm not stoppin' you."

"Kent, you're a Christian now." His words were a statement, not a question.

"Yeah, but I can be a Christian without goin' to church." His voice broke. "I ain't goin' there and have everybody comin' over and feelin' sorry for me! I don't care what you say!"

"Nobody's going to feel sorry for you or pity you, Kent," Danny said. "The people at church are your friends, like Lee Nelson and Pastor Reeves. They all feel badly that this has happened to you, but they will only want to help you."

Kent's lips began to quiver.

"I know what it'll be like. They'll come over an' try to think of somethin' to say, and all the time they'll be pitying me b-because I can't see!" Tears came to his eyes. "I'm not goin' over there and have that happen!" In desperation he reached out and grasped Danny's arm. "I won't go, Danny. I won't go anywhere."

"Kent," Danny answered sternly. "I agree that it will be hard for you to go to church the first time. But that's no reason for you not to go."

Bitterness curled the boy's mouth.

"I don't know why not."

"You can't stay in the house all the time. The sooner you get out among people the better it'll be for you." Danny glanced at his watch. "We've got to be on our way in ten minutes. There's no time for talking now, so go and get dressed." He spoke gently, but with a firmness that would not be disobeyed.

Reluctantly Kent got to his feet.

"Would somebody help me into the bedroom?" he asked plaintively.

"I've got to get my coat, Kent," Danny said. "I think you can manage."

Jill got to her feet quickly and started toward her brother, but Danny stopped her with a glance.

"Kent can make it to his room, Jill," he said. "You'd better go and get your coat and Bible. It's getting late."

The young girl stared at him, protest flaming in her eyes.

"But–"

Nevertheless, Kent stumbled forward uncertainly, groping his way to the bedroom. When he was gone Jill spoke to Danny.

"I could've taken him in there," she said.

"So could I, Jill." He reached over and put an arm around her. "In fact, that's what I really wanted to do, but it won't help Kent for us to wait on him all the time."

"But he–he might fall and hurt himself," she said numbly.

"We can't wait on him all his life," Danny explained as gently as possible. "We've got to do everything we can to teach him to take care of himself. OK?"

The blind boy's sister nodded, but without understanding.

* * *

The first Sunday night Jim that picked Connie up for church, the rest of the McCloud family had gone visiting somewhere, so she was home alone. The next Sunday, however, he had to go in and meet her folks. He had been afraid that would happen and got ready to go after her uneasily. Danny was sitting in the living room when he started for the front door shortly before seven o'clock.

"Well now, Jim," he said, "where do you think you're going?"

"To church."

"So early?"

Jim flushed scarlet. "Yeah," he acknowledged. "I–I've got a stop to make."

"I see." Danny laughed pleasantly. "Well, tell her to hurry so you're not late."

* * *

Connie came to the door in response to Jim's knock.

"Hello, Jim," she said. "Won't you come in while I get my coat?"

He stepped into the living room and looked around. Mrs. McCloud was sitting in an easy chair watching television and her husband was at the dining room table working on a pile of papers.

"Mother and Daddy," Connie said, "I'd like you to meet Jim Morgan."

Mr. McCloud got up and came over to shake his hand.

"We're glad to know you," he said.

It seemed to Jim that he actually meant it.

"We've been hearing quite a lot about you around here, young man."

This time it was Connie's turn to blush.

"Daddy!" she exclaimed.

"We're very glad to know you. To speak frankly, Jim, we're glad to have Connie go with a boy who takes her to church on Sunday night."

"That was one of our chief concerns when we moved here to Fairview. We were so very anxious that Fritz and Connie get in with a group of fine Christian kids."

Connie returned with her coat.

"I'm ready, Jim," she said.

They moved toward the door.

"Don't be late, Connie," her mother said. "You have school tomorrow, you know."

"We'll be home shortly after church."

"Yeah," Jim said. "I've got to be in before ten. Football curfew."

They had walked a block or so when Connie turned to Jim.

"I was so glad you asked me to go to church with you tonight. If you hadn't, I'd have had to stay home or go alone."

He glanced curiously at her.

"Don't your folks go to church on Sunday night?" he asked.

"Oh, they do sometimes." She spoke indifferently. "But today we had company at noon and Mom was so tired she didn't feel like going. And Daddy has to go out on a business trip early tomorrow morning, so he just *had* to go over some papers before he leaves."

Jim frowned thoughtfully.

"What about Fritz?" he asked. "Doesn't he go to church on Sunday night either?"

"Oh, Fritz. He usually leaves his studying until the last minute on weekends and has to stick to his books on Sunday night, or be half prepared for classes Monday morning."

Jim breathed deeply. They sure didn't have the same attitude toward church that Danny and Kay had. They seemed so casual – almost indifferent about it.

* * *

Danny and Kay had been waiting with some uneasiness for word from the welfare officer regarding Kent. At last Mr. Collins called and asked them to come to his office. When Danny said goodbye, Kent was standing there facing him.

"What'd he want?" he demanded.

"Who?"

"That was Mr. Collins, wasn't it?"

"Yes." Danny spoke slowly. "It was Mr. Collins." There was a short silence.

"I know what he wants, but he's not goin' to talk

me into it. I ain't goin' to no blind school! I don't care what he says!"

"He didn't say what they have decided," Danny answered. "He wants Kay and me to come down to his office this afternoon."

"I'm goin' along." There was defiance in the boy's voice. "I'm goin' to have something to say about whether I go to that stupid school or not."

"Mr. Collins asked us to come alone." Danny spoke quietly, but with conviction.

"He's not runnin' my life."

Danny did not argue with him, but when the time came for them to go, Kent was not along.

"Danny," Kay said, "what do you think they'll do with Kent?"

"They want what's best for him, and so do we. But I'm hoping they'll decide to leave him with us for a few more months."

"So do I. I hope we can keep him until his attitude changes a little."

Danny pulled into a parking space near the court-house and stopped.

"I was so sure that things would work out better for him once he accepted Christ," he said, "but he seems to be having almost as much difficulty in making the adjustment as before."

"He's having the same problem so many of us have when something like this happens," Kay went on. "He refuses to accept the fact that he's blind and that the situation isn't going to change. And he's not willing to let God take his life as it is and show him how to live a triumphant, happy Christian life in spite of his handicap."

"It won't be easy to do that," Danny said, "but he'll be so much happier when he does."

They went into the big building and up to the Welfare Office on the third floor. Mr. Collins got to his feet as they entered and spoke cordially to them.

"I've been wanting to get in touch with you for the last several days," he said, "but we've been so busy I haven't been able to do it until now."

"Have you come to a decision regarding Kent?"

"That's what I want to talk to you about. As you know, our interest is the same as yours. We all want to do what's best for the boy."

"Danny said the same thing a few minutes ago," Kay put in. "We would like very much to keep him with us for awhile in an effort to get him to change his attitude. But we are quite willing to do whatever you and the people at the school for the blind feel is best for him."

Mr. Collins leaned forward, pressing his fingers together thoughtfully.

"We appreciate your attitude, and your concern for Kent. We know that he has caused you all sorts of trouble and has been anything but kind and loving, but still you've stayed by him."

"Kent has needed us." Danny spoke simply. "And he has allowed Christ to work in his life."

The welfare worker nodded.

"You two put your faith to work," he said. There was a serious set to his mouth. "When you talk about your religion, a person can't help but listen." Then, as though afraid they would continue to testify to him, he went on quickly. "If it weren't for you, we would insist on putting Kent in the school immediately. But we have decided that if you want to keep him until the beginning of the second semester, it will be all right with us."

Kay sighed her relief.

"Oh, thank you. Thank you very much."

"But if he should become difficult, or if you should feel that you can no longer do anything for him, we'll take him at any time."

When Danny and Kay returned home half an hour or so later, Kent was waiting for them at the front door.

"I don't care what they said," Kent said. "I won't go to that old school!"

Kay put a hand on his shoulder affectionately.

"You don't have to go right away."

His young body stiffened, and disbelief crept into his voice.

"What?"

"You don't have to go to school until the start of the next semester."

The blind boy took a deep breath.

"Are you sure?"

"That's what Mr. Collins said. Of course, we're all anxious to have you go because it's so important that you learn to read braille and finish your education.

But we're glad that you're going to get to stay with us for a few more months."

Tears trickled down the boy's cheeks.

"At–at least I don't have to leave before Christmas," he said.

Impulsively Kay hugged him.

"Kent," she said, "it won't make any difference when you go to the school for the blind, as far as your being with us for Christmas is concerned. This is your home. Not only now, but for as long as you want it to be. We want you to feel free to come back here for Christmas, or at any other time you can."

For a moment or two his lips trembled.

"You–you mean that?" His thin young voice broke. "You're not just saying it so I–I won't feel so bad about goin' away?"

"No, I'm not." She stooped beside him. "Kent, this is your home as much as it's ours. You belong here."

"You couldn't mean that," he said. "Not after all the things I've done and–"

Tenderly she grasped his shoulders.

"Kent," she said, "have I ever lied to you?"

There was a brief hesitation. "No, I–I guess not."

"I'm not lying to you now. You and Jill are part of our family. We love you as though you were our own flesh and blood."

Danny spoke up quickly.

"That's right, Kent. Our home is yours just as long as you want it to be."

Kent pulled in a long, deep breath and slowly expelled the air.

"I–I thought that if I–I went to that school for the blind I–I'd never be able to come back here again."

With that he started to cry, unashamedly.

Kay swept him into her arms, and for the space of a minute or two their tears mingled.

THE DANNY ORLIS SERIES

The Danny Orlis series, by Bernard Palmer, delivers a blend of adventure, mystery, and suspense through various settings—from the Canadian wilderness to Guatemalan jungles. Danny Orlis, an adept outdoorsman, skilled athlete, and committed Christian, employs his quick thinking, calm bravery, and biblical solutions to confront everyday problems and hair-raising dangers. Early stories focus on Danny navigating school life, sports, and outdoor challenges, while in later books, Danny and his wife Kay provide wisdom and guidance to youngsters facing lifelike situations and challenges. Having sold over two million copies, this series has made Palmer a renowned author in Christian youth literature. Palmer is also the author of the Felicia Cartright series and various other series for Christian youth.

AVAILABLE FROM WWW.ANEKOPRESS.COM